Don Malott

The Munchkin Battles the Minotaur

A NOVEL IN THE MUNCHKIN CHRONICLES

This is a work of fiction. This is not about you, him, her, or anyone else you think it is. The author made this stuff up. Except that part you think is about you... it totally is. Just kidding. Seriously, any person, place, or thing in this book comes from the author's weird imagination and questionable sense of humor.

1
THE MUNCHKIN BEGINS

"Are you sure this is a good idea?" I asked Brother Damien for the second time.

The last time they asked me to have an impromptu sparring session I'd sort of broken a couple of people. It wasn't my fault. Really, it wasn't. People just move so slowly.

But it didn't go over well. I ended up receiving a lot of lectures about *discipline* and *reasonable* levels of force by people who obviously had never had three grown men charging at them with clubs. Sure, the clubs were padded, but that didn't mean they didn't hurt. And what was the point of training, anyway, unless you tried your hardest?

But here we were, less than a month later, and he wanted me to fight again for the benefit of some unseen evaluators. And this time I was only supposed to fight one guy.

Brother Damien sighed again, and I could feel his concern. "Yes, Anne, you fight in twenty minutes. Go get ready."

With that, I left his office and went back to my room. There I dressed in my black yoga pants and a sports bra. Then I put on my fighting leathers and a form-fitting The Tick t-shirt because I was feeling nigh invulnerable. Okay, that might also be to tweak Brother Damien a little. It was worth another lecture on *decorum* to have a little fun. After all, isn't that what girls are supposed to want to have?

Fifteen minutes later I was completely dressed, relaxed, and feeling confident. I had curled my hair into tight bun so there would be nothing to grab. I wasn't really worried about anyone being strong enough to use my hair as a weapon, and it tended to pull out in any case, but it beat having another lecture on *preparedness*. It also beat looking like I had mange for the couple of days it took for my hair to grow back.

I did one last check in the mirror and was satisfied with the result. Looking back at me in the mirror was a slightly smaller-than-average height, too skinny, harmless blonde, with pretty hair, blue eyes, and not nearly enough chest. I looked just like your average teenager. I was anything but that. Um, I mean, I was five foot four, clocked in at maybe one hundred pounds if my hair was wet, and could use a little more chest, but that's not what I meant. What I meant was that I was way stronger and faster than I looked.

I had briefly considered using stakes to hold my slightly-longer-than shoulder-length hair up, but that would be cheating since they could be used as weapons and I was told no weapons were allowed. Besides, due to some cosmic fluke in the universe, the bun actually looked good for once. So, no weapons, no shoes, no belt, just me. Well, I did have on a necklace Daddy had bought it for me in Saudi on his last business trip. It was a beautiful gold chain with a small cross that I'd put on it later. It was all I had left of him and I never took it off.

Then I made my way to the practice arena. It looked pretty much the same as it did every day. There were padded mats on the floors and walls, a small area above for spectators, and not much else. The only differences between today and every other day was there were maybe ten people in the area waiting to see me spar, and the racks that held the practice weapons had been removed.

I spent a couple of minutes stretching, although I didn't need to do that anymore. It did give me time, though, to observe the people who were there to observe me: an odd mix of old and distinguished-looking men and women, and young, less distinguished, but more dangerous-looking men.

Finally, the south door opened, and my opponent walked in wearing a look of contempt. *Okay, this is new.* He didn't actually walk in, he just sort of appeared in a pop of air. I let out a little squeak before I could stop myself.

Yeah, I get it. I am a girl. I sometimes squeak when I'm surprised. Get over it. It doesn't make me weak. In fact, maybe the opposite because it's caused people in the past to underestimate me.

But back to my story.

As he entered the room, it got colder. I don't mean it felt colder or I got a chill or anything like that. The room literally got a few degrees colder. I studied him as he looked at me. My eyes were maybe level with the top of his chest, so, typical of the guys that I had trained with. He looked thin but not particularly athletic. But he moved with a grace that I envied. Then he stared at me and his eyes seemed to look into my soul; to this day I cannot recall their color, only that I couldn't look away from them. I was frozen.

He appeared to be about forty, and he was unmistakably cruel. Anger and disdain dripped off him like a brown stink and I could tell instantly he was there not just to hurt me. This guy wanted to dominate me, to take my will, to make me quit. He wasn't there to fight me. He was there to own and possess me. It was really freaky.

I still couldn't move, but he didn't have that problem. He moved, fast, faster than anyone I've ever seen. He was on me before I had a chance to blink—I mean, if my eyes were working and I could have blinked—and he threw me ten feet into the padded mats on the wall. Before I could even slide down, his left hand was on my throat and he was holding me in the air, choking me, my feet dangling off the ground, my blood oozing out where his fingertips had dug in.

His eyes bored into mine and he spoke in a soft, ugly voice. "They should not have sent you to me, little girl, but I am glad they did. I will drink you down and make you mine. I will teach you pain such as you have never known. Only when you no longer beg for death will I consider allowing it."

I couldn't help it. With what breath I had left, I giggled a little. I mean, sure, he had me dead to rights. He could have taken me out in those brief seconds, and there wouldn't have been a thing I could do about it. But instead of ending the fight, he soliloquized! What was he, the poster child for a bad villain?

I didn't waste time telling him what a stupid thing he'd done. Instead, as he looked surprised at my giggle, he loosened his hold a bit and I slammed my left wrist into the inside of his left hand, broke his grip, opened my hand and stabbed my fingers into his throat. As he dropped me, I rammed a knee into his groin, and a right forearm to his forehead as he bent forward, then finished it all up with a left hook to his stupid jaw. That, at least, should shut him up.

He staggered back a few feet and I thought he was going to struggle for breath, but he merely regained his balance and charged me. Then it was really on. For the next uncountable minutes, we went at it. He was faster and stronger than me—I mean, a *lot* faster and stronger. I felt like a teenager fighting an adult.

Yeah, I get the irony, I *was* a teenager fighting an adult. Fortunately for me, he didn't have my training. He evidently relied on his natural abilities instead of training.

I managed to slip the worst of his attacks and catch the ones I couldn't dodge on forearms, hips, etc. They still hurt like the dickens but at least they were not incapacitating. It's funny how often people think that blocking a blow or channeling it to a less sensitive area means it won't hurt. It does. A lot. But I had been training for a couple of years now and I had a pretty good grasp of pain. My instructors weren't gentle.

Anyway, in between his onslaughts I managed a few blows to his more sensitive areas and hurt him a little here and there. But I was losing. I knew it. He knew it. I knew he knew it. He knew I knew it. He wasn't getting tired and nothing I did seemed to hurt him for more than a few seconds. I was healing almost as fast as he was, but my stamina was not infinite, and his seemed to be. I was starting to slow and more of his blows were landing. For those of you who haven't been in a lot of fights, you can think of my predicament as *not good.*

Then I got lucky. As I barely dodged his swipe at my throat, my necklace popped out and my little cross flared up like it was its own sun. Even the gold of the necklace glowed. The light made him jump straight back and he grabbed at his left hand, which seemed to be badly burned where it had touched my necklace.

"Enough!" someone shouted loudly from the observation area, and my opponent staggered as he was shot with needles by two men who seemed to move almost before the shout was finished. Wow. They were fast.

He staggered for a few steps and then slid to the floor while men rushed in and wrapped him up in stuff that resembled duct tape.

I wanted to drop to my knees in exhaustion. I wanted to curl up in a ball and cry. I was beaten, tired, sore, and I had failed. I couldn't have taken this guy in a fair fight. If my necklace hadn't done whatever it just did, I'd have lost.

I was a failure, and worse, I was a cheat. I didn't mean to be a cheater but that did not change anything. Tears began flowing but I was not going to sob in front of the crowd that had gathered. Instead, I held my head high, bowed toward the observers, and exited the gym with what little dignity I had left. Then I marched into my room and took the hottest shower I could. While the aches and pains melted away, the tears came again, but this time I didn't try to stop them.

I was a failure.

I was still on the shower floor trying to let the shame and failure wash away in the scalding water when I heard a soft knock on the bedroom door. I didn't get out. I didn't even get up. I just shouted, "*What?*"

The reply has hesitant. "Brother Damien would like to see you in his office when you're finished."

I gathered what was left of my dignity, and replied, "Fine. Please tell him I will be there in thirty minutes."

After my surly reply, I stood up and began doing all those fun things girls do to get ready that boys do not know about. Sure, boys like the results, so maybe they can just shut up when we take a little longer to get ready than they do.

I knocked on Brother Damien's door twenty-eight minutes later. I did not want to be disrespectful even if I was going to be thrown out in the next few minutes.

Brother Damien called me in and was seated behind his desk as always. "Take a seat, Anne. I imagine you're sore and tired. Would you like something to drink?" he asked while cleaning his glasses.

"I'm fine, thank you." I sat down and got right to it. "Let me get right to it, Brother Damien. I failed. I cheated. I didn't mean to cheat, really, I didn't. I get it. Rules are rules. I'd like another chance, please." I realized I was starting to sound whiny and quickly stopped. I would not beg. I also wouldn't let the tears fall that were trying so hard to break free.

"You think you failed, Anne?" Brother Damien asked with something like shock in his voice. "You went toe-to-toe with a *vampire*. His gaze couldn't hold you. His will didn't break you. You even managed to hurt him. I would say you were nothing short of extraordinary today. That little test was never something you were supposed to pass. No one can beat a vampire one-on-one without weapons." He paused for a second. "Well, maybe one man can, depending on the vampire, but he has a lot more training than you do. An hour ago, you didn't believe in vampires, and you still almost managed to beat one."

"Then what was the point?" I asked, near tears. "Were you just trying to break me? Teach me that I can't do the job? Get me killed for nothing? Have an easy excuse to throw me out?"

Brother Damien shook his head and looked sad; however, his voice was very firm. "Partly yes to all of that. I care about you, Anne. A lot of us here do. You were never in serious danger of dying. Accidents do happen, but you may have noticed how quickly that foul creature was taken down once the signal was given." He paused to clean his glasses again. "The test was to show my superiors you weren't ready. That you needed at least another year of training, if not more. I was told they need someone immediately for a special job. I didn't want that someone to be you."

"And?" I replied, feeling horribly confused and betrayed.

"And it backfired on me. You impressed a great many people this morning." He paused for a second. It was evident that he didn't like what he had to say next, but his duty won out. "You are now officially employed by the Church, if you wish. You can hunt the shadows in the dark, you can help stem the tide of evil. For now, you would be one of our Shadow Hunters. In time, and with a lot more training, you could even be a Light Bringer." As he spoke, his sadness fell away and he became more impassioned, but then, of course, he paused to clean his glasses again, which ruined the effect. "But I would ask you to wait. I can get you an extension. I can get you more time to grow with us. More time to get better prepared. More time to be a child. They can find someone else for this mission."

"But I'm not a child," I replied sadly. "I am an orphan. I stopped being a child when my parents died." Tears began to flow and this time I didn't care. "I don't really have anything but you and the Church right now. I have no parents, no brothers or sisters. I need this. I need something. If this isn't it, then fine, but I will not quit before I get started. Please, let me try."

Brother Damien looked very sad. But he also knew that when I made up my mind there was no going back. "Very well," he said in a resigned tone of voice. "Against my better judgement I will accept you into the Order of Light. The Church will sell your possessions. You will lose all ties with the outside world. No contact with any of the people you used to know; you can only put them in danger now. An account will be set up for you for expenses. Your parents left you a fair amount of money, so you won't starve between missions. Besides, we are paid well for stopping the Shadows. You, in turn, will be well paid for each mission. Plus, the Church will provide you armor, weapons, and expenses while in the field.

"One last thing, Anne. Our operatives take a new name with their new identity. You will of course always be Anne to me. But you will be known in the Church by something else so that as few people as possible know who you really are. This will be your name for the rest of your life. Take your time to think of the one you want."

I smiled. "I suppose Taser Face would be a copyright infraction or something. Too bad. That would really strike fear into my enemies." At Brother Damien's frown I quickly toned down my sense of humor. "Okay, Brother. No need for me to think on this. Call me 'Munchkin.'"

2
THE WOODS

I was excited for my first mission and really eager to get started, and the three-hour drive through traffic left me nearly bursting with energy. By the time my driver, George, dropped me off about twenty miles north of Chicago, I was fighting myself to remain calm. We were in a small lot near a fairly large wood. The temperature was in the low seventies, there were no clouds, a pleasant breeze was blowing, and we were far enough outside of town that I could even see a few stars. It was a wonderful beginning.

George was going on about something like he had for the last couple of hours. He was a nice man, but chatty. I did not want chatty right now. I wanted to be starting the mission. Oh, well, I guess I could have driven myself, so it was my fault anyway. But the Order had explained that it was better having George drive me than trusting that I could leave the car alone for any length of time this close to Chicago, and have it intact, or even there when I returned. I was regretting giving in on that. Driving myself would have cut down on the inevitable chitchat and advice George felt that a pretty, blond-haired eighteen-year-old girl needed when getting dropped off by a woods in the middle of the night.

And while we are on the topic, me calling myself pretty is not some vanity thing. I was starting to look like Mama, who everyone had said was gorgeous. I doubted I'd ever have her sense of poise, calm, and understanding of her place in the world, but I did have a slightly larger chest. That's humor for those of you keeping track. Also, I got enough stupid looks from even stupider boys to know where I stood on their "I am going to make a fool of myself" scale.

"You sure I shouldn't go with you, Miss Anne?" George asked for the third time, interrupting my thoughts again. "I don't mind. The Brothers just told me that I should make sure you have a ride. They didn't say anything about leaving you all alone in the woods at night."

I tried to be patient with him. I really did. But I was excited, and my patience and sarcasm definitely run in opposite directions. I was supposed to be trying to monitor that but, in general, sarcasm was my go-to move. "I'll be fine, George. What could possibly happen to a blond, teenaged girl walking alone through the forest on a dark and cloudy night? It is not as if I'm carrying a basket to grandma's house or wearing a bikini or meeting my boyfriend near a haunted cemetery. I am almost completely cliché-free. Besides, I'm supposed to be looking for someone abducting young people who are alone in the forest.

You know . . . someone abducting stupid kids. If I went into the woods with a large, grandfatherly-looking man carrying a poorly concealed Glock 9, I don't think I would fit that profile very well.

"Now, you go back to the Motel 6 we passed a few miles back, smoke a couple of those cigarettes you don't think anyone can smell, and wait for my call. This shouldn't take more than a few hours. By then I'll either have this wrapped up, be excited and insufferable, or," I paused for dramatic effect and made my eyes wide and spooky, "be dead. And you'll have a nice, quiet ride back to the Bend."

George looked stricken and I felt awful.

Mama had always said no one got my sense of humor and I should probably stop trying to be funny. Then again, Daddy always countered with why would anybody want to be friends with people who had no sense of humor, so, you know, half full.

I decided to go with Mama on this one and told George, "Seriously, I know you are trying to protect me and that's sweet. It really is. It is also really not necessary. I have been training for a long time for this. I'll be fine. When I get done, I will give you a call to come get me and we can discuss better concealment for your gun, and maybe switching to vaping on the ride back. Seriously, we're just outside of Chicago, George. Everyone knows there are no guns in Chicago, so you, a large black man concealing a pistol, with a blond-haired girl in the back seat, is kind of conspicuous."

With those rousing words of assurance, I got out of the black Lincoln Town Car—which in no way looked like an unmarked government vehicle—and made my way into the forest before he could argue any more about coming with me.

I went into the woods about a hundred yards and stopped for a few seconds to acclimatize myself to the surroundings. Yes, acclimatize. There is nothing about being young, or blond, that means I cannot have a decent vocabulary. My parents were so insistent about me speaking well that I always amazed adults—and had few friends my age.

All of my senses were way more acute than a typical human, but a moment or two to let my eyes fully adjust and my nerves to calm down seemed like a good idea. This was definitely a rush job type of assignment, but not so much that I couldn't spare a couple of minutes to avoid stumbling in the dark. As I leaned against an old tree that I thought was a birch but probably wasn't, I replayed the conversation Brother Damien and I had about the mission in my head.

Brother Damien, in spite of his poorly chosen name, was a kind-looking man who fit nearly every stereotype for professor and none of the stereotypes for a Brother. He was tall, too thin, with a salt-and-pepper beard, expensive-looking wire-rimmed glasses and the inevitable tweed jacket with leather patches at the elbows. He sat behind a big, heavy desk that seemed to be more clutter than desk, smoothed back his unkempt hair while searching for the best way to tell me I probably was not ready for this, again.

Brother Damien had been with me since the accident and thought of me much more as little Anne lying broken in a hospital bed than the stone-cold monster-killing Munchkin that I was rapidly becoming.

"Are you sure you are ready for this, Anne?" he asked again. "I can put in for a few months more training for you. I really think that would be for the best."

"Brother Damien," I replied, just short of exasperated. "I appreciate the way you've been looking out for me. I really do. But you keep telling me this mission requires a teenager. I'm pretty sure I would have noticed if there were any other teenagers around here training with me. Since I seem to be the only one, in fact the only person who's getting trained, I think I am the most qualified person for this, uh, whatever this is. Besides, I haven't been outside the building more than a dozen times in the last year."

Tears started to well up and I fiercely cracked down on them. Okay, that was a slight exaggeration. I willed them not to come and they came anyway. I cry. I am an eighteen-year-old girl who cries a lot. Get over it. It doesn't make me weak. Maybe a little dehydrated at times, but not weak!

"Someone is needed for this, and I've been chosen by the Order. So, can we please move past the part where you try to talk me out of it again and get to the part where you tell me what this 'it' is?"

He shot me one last look as if he was going to try to talk me out of it, hesitated for moment, and began. "Over the last month seven teenagers have gone missing from a forest just north of Chicago. At first, no one noticed the number. The woods cover more than one jurisdiction and so it wasn't reported as seven missing children. Three different police departments were each conducting their own investigations. Some of the children were reported as 'missing,' and some as potential runaways. We are talking about a very common gathering place for teens who want to have some fun without adults around. It is also a popular camping site, so people get lost there every summer.

"Things changed last week. The daughter of a local politician went there with some friends and vanished. Literally vanished. Her friends said she walked off to be alone for a few minutes and just disappeared. Her father had enough pull to get a search party organized. Dogs and trackers followed what they thought was her path for a couple of miles and then all signs of her disappeared. All of Chicago started to take at least some notice, and the various police departments began comparing notes. Our contact at one of these departments let us know something very unusual might be happening. We've been asked by the Chicago diocese to look into this for them."

"The Chicago diocese?" I asked. "Why is the Church looking for a missing girl? Do they think this is demonic or something? Um . . . I'm not really trained for that sort of thing. I've been more focused on the 'put an arrow through them at a distance' or 'beat the crap out of them up close' part of my training."

"No," he replied while removing his already clean glasses to clean them again, "not demonic. Seven teenagers so far. We are expecting seven more before this finally stops. Every seven years for the last one hundred twenty-six years, around the end of summer, fourteen teenagers disappear. A few months later their skeletons are found with what appear to be auroch teeth marks on them. This is the first time we have heard about it in time to potentially stop it. We scan the news religiously, if you'll excuse the pun, but we've never been able to get the abductions verified in time to actually do anything about them."

"Auroch?" I replied with a disbelieving smile. "Are you telling me that a bull, over six feet tall, weighing a couple thousand pounds, and extinct as of around five hundred years ago is traveling around eating kids, and no one has seen it? Did they find giant bull prints or something? I don't really follow the news much but even I would have heard of that. How does this bull even get around, by Miura? And how could he afford one anyway? Lamborghinis are expensive." I laughed at the last part, but, as usual, my sense of humor was not appreciated.

"This is not funny, young lady," Brother Damien said with something close to anger.

Wow! I did strike a nerve. Everyone said I was the only one who could damage his calm, but until now I thought Brother Damien getting upset was mostly a myth. You know, like "good-tasting fake meat" or "low-calorie ice cream." It appears that I have more skill than I thought. My reverie almost made me miss the rest of his dialogue. *Pay Attention, Munchkin!* I thought.

"Fourteen children disappear every seven years," he continued. "There is no sign of them for months. The skeletons are just found later, in grounds that were already well-searched, and are brought to Italy for examination. The parents are never told of this because there is no way to explain the damage to their bodies. They are usually just told there is no hope for finding their child, and the searches are called off. It is truly a godforsaken time. But this time we can stop it. Or rather, perhaps you can."

Again, a pause to clean the glasses. I wonder if it is for dramatic effect or a nervous habit. Again, *PAY ATTENTION!*

"About one hundred twenty-six years ago there was an archeological dig in Crete," he finally continued. "Nothing new there. There is almost always someone digging up things best left buried. This expedition was supposedly to find a famous maze that was lost to history long ago. Expeditioners promised to do the search without disturbing any relics or ancient structures, so they were allowed into very sensitive and historically important areas. It was incredibly stupid but evidently, they had a lot of pull from some anonymous benefactor. Sadly, they found something, or at least we think they did.

"One night, screams and the sounds of a fight were heard. Two graduate students were found brutally beaten; there were bull tracks by their bodies. Searchers didn't find any tracks leading to or away from the bodies. All they found was an old rock with a double-bit ax broken in two a few feet away. Police were called and the site was shut down. A month later two children disappeared nearby, and the site was permanently closed. Over the next few weeks twelve more children disappeared. Eventually, their bones were discovered at the site with auroch bite marks on them. Fourteen more skeletons have appeared every seven years at approximately the same time of year since then. Unfortunately, we never find out about it until after the children's bones are found. The skeletons have come from all over the world, both genders, rich and poor.

"One common factor is that they are always children's

bones—interestingly enough, the definition of 'child' does vary by continent and region. Secondly, the disappearances always happen roughly this time of year. It is hard to tell exactly when the children go missing, because we have to identify the bones, and then backtrack to get the dates. Anyway, the bones are found a few months after the abduction, with auroch teeth marks on them, and the disappearances stop again until seven years later."

"Soooo," I said slowly, "it's not an auroch. It's a Minotaur? A Minotaur that can travel the world unseen, is at least a hundred and twenty-six years old, and just happens to be taking children outside of Chicago?"

"Exactly. This is the first time we've ever found out about the abductions before they stop. Gear up. There are several maps of the area for you to study on the way. Take whatever you think you might need. A driver will be here for you in an hour. Any questions?"

"Do we happen to have a magic ball of string?" I asked with a smile. When Brother Damien gave me his long-suffering look, I turned and headed for the weapons room, muttering, "If we only had a holocaust cloak. Now that would be something."

With that cheery thought, I put enough gear to last a month in a firefight in downtown Beirut, along with a ton of energy bars into my go-bag that doubled as a backpack. I always overpacked even when I was just a normal girl, going on trips with her family. I've never found myself thinking, "Thank goodness I forgot that," so over-packing seemed to be the better policy.

3

BACK TO THE WOODS

Anyway, back to the woods. It quickly became almost daylight bright and the colors of the woods dimmed as my eyes adjusted, and I began to weapon up. Yes, I know I could have had my weapons ready when I got out of the car. But, again, George was a middle-aged black man driving a young white girl through Chicago. I figured I was tempting fate enough and left the majority of my weapons in my go-bag. Besides, I was already wearing most of my preferred fighting gear and could handle most threats sans weapons.

Unless the Minotaur turned out to be a vampire, I thought, cursing myself and my over-confidence.

A couple of minutes later and I was as ready as I thought I could be. My BDUs were stylish and definitely not typical. They were black, with a lot of pockets and looked more teenaged Goth than adult badass. My undergarments were bullet resistant. Typhon, if you are curious, with ballast panels sewn into the base layer. Over them I wore my synthetic leather pants with a few surprises sewn in. I usually wear real leather but since I was supposedly bull hunting, I thought that would be insensitive. A black t-shirt that asks the universal question "Can you shoot like a girl?" in white letters, and a synthetic leather jacket with tons of pockets completed my look. It wasn't cold outside, and I rarely got cold anyway, but a jacket gave me more protection, and more pockets.

My favorite black slippers completed the look. Contact with the ground and silence were much more important to me on this mission than potentially bruised feet. Besides, I liked them, and they were really comfortable. I had some old-school army boots and even some Doc Martens that I also loved, but practical considerations won the day. My bruises would heal as fast as I got them, noise was forever.

I gave myself one last check. Sure, my look was way over the top but with some black lipstick and eyeliner, I could pass for Goth with ease.

For those of you who like a lot of details, I will tell you that I slipped long knives into the front of the pants and into each holder. The knives had flat, black hilts and the blades were coated with a water-soluble paint so the silvered edge would not shine, but the paint would almost instantly come off when touched by water or blood, so the silver would still be effective. At least that's what they told me. I was still having some trouble with that thought. Sure, I'd just fought a vampire, but I had spent a lot more time believing they were myths than I had knowing they were real.

Anyway, the knives in the front of my pants were almost invisible when properly inserted. All my knives were better for fighting than throwing but balanced enough that they would throw at least decently in a pinch. Around my neck was my pretty necklace with a silver cross that doubled (tripled?) as a vampire ward and garrote. A black wool cap so I could tuck my hair in was next.

I leave my hair slightly longer than shoulder-length, but I have had it grabbed enough in sparring practice to know that having it grabbed wouldn't affect me much. I can't be controlled as easily as a normal person with a hair grab, but it still hurts when it comes out, and it takes forever for it to grow back evenly. Shooting gloves with silver studs sewn in and covered by a black, Velcro strap, a couple of tiny surprises in the pockets and my go-bag was nearly empty except for my medication which I take three times a day, energy bars (gross, but much needed with my metabolism), a water bottle, purification tablets, and my baby.

I brought her out and looked at her lovingly. She was a beauty—at least to me. She was a short bow with modified crossbow limbs and a nearly two hundred-pound draw. I did mention I was a lot stronger than your typical eighteen-year-old girl, didn't I? She was dark blue (blue being the best color) with a dark blue string and very slightly lighter nock. I could carry her easily attached to my hip or on my back but typically left her in the go-bag as I didn't want her snagging if I had to run. With her were twenty modified arrows that were as stiff as crossbow bolts and fit into slots on my bag for ease of reach. Screwed on the bolts were modified mechanical blades. They were similar to typical Rage blades, but sharper, silver edged, and the shock collar was retooled by hand so there was zero chance of failure. Rage blades don't fail out of the box, but why take the chance?

Weaponed-up, feeling appropriately dangerous, and now totally adjusted to the sights and sounds of nature, I headed into the woods for what I assumed was going to be a long night of probably fruitless searching. After all, the Minotaur left no tracks. It did not even leave any sign unless it actually took someone, and the forest was supposed to be empty except for me. If I found a broken stone with a double-edged ax engraved into it, I'd know I was on the right track, but I'd also be too late. That wasn't much to go on. I was more hoping to be "found" and "surprised" than to have any luck tracking the thing.

At least it was a pleasant night and the forest, while not old growth, had enough trails and walking paths through it that stumbling or bruising my feet was not going to be an issue. The trees felt comforting to me and I heard sounds of small animals rustling around me. There were very few insects, but they typically didn't bite me much anyway, which I chalked up to the drugs I was taking. It felt good to be outside again and I was as much reveling in the solitude and darkness as I was searching for clues. Sure, time was of the essence, and people's lives were at stake, but I couldn't help but enjoy being outdoors and alone for the first time in months.

Somewhere around an hour later I stopped to eat a power bar and take a sip of water when I heard them.

Are you freaking kidding me? I thought.

I mean, yeah, boys are stupid. But how freaking stupid can they be? The woods were closed, and people had gone missing and these idiots had evidently decided it was a nice time to enjoy a little getaway.

I stopped and listened carefully for a minute and I heard three distinct voices yelling "Chad! Come on, man, this isn't funny! Chad? We have to be going soon! Not cool, man!"

Well, this certainly changed things. I couldn't exactly go up to the boys dressed like this to get more information. I needed to find Chad before he was number eight on the disappearance list. I also needed those boys to go away. I also needed more information. Finally, I needed to find Chad's home address so I could slap his parents for giving him that name. Did they just think to themselves: "How can I guarantee my child grows up to be a douche? What name will secure him being an a-hole?" Yeesh, people. Come on. Really? Chad?

Anyway, I made my way over to the boys' campsite as silently as I could. Even in the woods at night this meant I made no sounds that a normal person could hear. I can be very quiet when I want to be, even moving at a decent pace.

The boys had gathered back by their meager fire and I settled in to listen to a couple of minutes of "What do you think? What do *you* think? Should we leave him? We need help? We're in so much trouble. What do we do now?"

Okay, so, as per usual, teenaged boys had nothing worthwhile to say, and were just wasting my time with prattle. They mostly went back and forth between being scared and trying to be brave and "manly." It was kind of like being on a date. Anyway, time to chase them off so I could find Chad. My voice was not low enough to scare anyone; it was on the high end of the scale to start with, and Daddy always said that when I yelled only dogs could hear most of it, so I settled for throwing a large stick about fifteen feet to the left of their campsite. When that accomplished nothing except more inane comments and accelerated heartbeats (yes, I can hear heartbeats, even at a distance) I threw another one fifteen feet right of the campsite and one straight into their fire. Finally, they ran off into the night, probably to end up with sprained ankles. Not even I run through woods at night if I can help it. Boys!

So, I went to the campsite and put out the small fire the idiot boys had left. No point in letting the forest burn down just because boys are stupid. Then I started following tracks. I quickly eliminated the ones who were running away and focused on Chad's. Fifteen feet out, ironically not far from the second limb I threw, Chad had dropped an empty beer bottle. Douche.

I picked it up and smelled it to get his scent, then put it in my bag to recycle later. He'd stopped again, five feet later. This time to pee. It looked like he was trying to spell his name or something—again, boys, ugh. Then things got interesting. He had looked around and then headed deeper into the woods. He'd made frequent stops over the next quarter of mile or so as if he was looking or listening for something.

Twenty feet later or so his tracks just disappeared by an old tree. I approached the area slowly and circled the tree. It did not appear to be anything special, just an old tree, large, maybe oak, maybe not, and thickly solid. I pushed against it in several spots but did not feel any hidden entrances or levers to pull that would lead to strange, underground passages or anything. Crap, failure. Signs of Chad had just vanished. There was nothing left to do but make sure I did not leave any of my tracks and headed deeper into the woods, hopefully to find a new lead.

"Hail, fair maiden, either I mistake in most lucid sight, or I dream fair upon the night. Such a vision of beauty and battle, chasing Chad, the fool, most foully taken by the one who looks like cattle."

I let out a small squeak and drew a dagger while spinning toward the voice. *Okay. This is definitely weird,* I thought, trying to calm myself. First, nothing sneaks up on me. And I mean nothing short of a vampire or ghost. That is, if there are ghosts. I know there are vampires and I'm not a fan, but I wasn't sure about ghosts. And I am also not bragging when I say I do not get sneaked up on. I can hear freaking heartbeats and see in almost complete darkness. But someone *had* snuck up on me and was sitting on a stump not two feet away. He had *not* been there a second ago. I would swear to that.

I took a moment to examine him while composing myself. He was shorter than me, with lean muscles that spoke of the quick and fluid movement of a fighter. His eyes were a piercing blue and his hair was just long enough to look unruly without being unkempt. He was maybe twenty with a friendly face and a nose just a tad too big for him to be classically handsome. Cute, maybe, but not handsome. Definitely not that. He had a short sword and knife on his belt set up for cross draw and what looked like a shillelagh perched by his legs. The handles on all his weapons were smooth with use so these were not decorations. He wore old jeans, well-worn work boots, and a flannel shirt.

Oh, and he had long, pointy ears. I mean really long, like bat wings or something. Maybe I should have led with that.

"And you are?" I asked, centering myself for the probable fight. After all, this dude came out of nowhere, knew about Chad, and looked for all the world like he had no fear of a well-armed, if small woman. And even small, I was quite a bit taller than him. He might be five-foot tall, but that would be at the top end.

"I am that merry wanderer of the night. I jest to Oberon and make him smile. When I—"

"Stop. Just stop," I countered, smiling. "I get it. You are pretending to be Robin Goodfellow. The Puck. Well, Mr. The Puck, I am a little busy here. I have a missing douche to find and a Minotaur to battle. I do not have time for any more myths or legends right now, so unless you can be of some value, I will bid thee go away."

"Ah, the scorn of the young maiden. So perfect in its derision. So certain in its ability to wound. So convinced she knows all, yet so unknowing. So—"

"So tired of this conversation?" I interrupted, rolling my eyes.

"Seriously, Mr. The Puck. I am trying to be nice like Mama taught me, but you are pushing it. There are lives at stake here," I heard the beginning of a whine in my voice which annoyed me, "so please, be of assistance or be gone."

Mr. The Puck smiled at me in a way that made me very uncomfortable. It was not predation or avarice but something close to each. I have been getting more and more of these looks lately from men and they made me nervous and unsure—or mad. Yeah, that's it, mad.

"I'll offer you a trade then, fair maiden. There is one thing the Puck loves more than all else. Offer me this in a trade and I will tell you where to find the one you seek."

"Look Mr. The Puck," I said with some heat. "You're cute and all for a much, much older guy, but please don't go all Epstein on me. I would hate to have you 'accidentally' hang yourself out here."

"You wound me, fair one," Mr. The Puck said sadly, "Not all males are the disgusting creatures that seem so common in your realm." He stopped for a moment to ponder while I raised my eyebrows in a "really?" expression. "Okay," he continued, "maybe most males are. But not the Puck!" he said with heat. "I am merely asking for a story. Tell me how one so young and so fair comes to be in the woods at night, armed like a warrior, with the grace of an Amazon, and with the poise and confidence to speak so to the Puck without fear. Tell me true a tale that seems most interesting, fair maiden, and I will in turn aid thee. A fair bargain, the better the tale, the greater the aid."

I thought it over, but I didn't really have much choice. One, I had no clue how to find Chad, and b, if a creature out of legend is going to pop into existence in front of me, offer help, and I am going to keep believing I am sane, I might as well play along and pretend this is all normal. "Okay, Mr. The Puck. I tell you my tale and you grant me the following: You tell me how to find the Minotaur and rescue Chad. If I cannot get wherever they are myself, you take me there. You do not warn him. You help me rescue Chad, and you grant me all the aid you can. You do nothing in any manner to hinder my mission. Agreed?"

"You bargain like a Fae, fair one, which I suppose only makes sense," he said with a pleasant smile. "I cannot give you all you ask. I will counter with this. Should I like your tale I will get you as close to the Minotaur's location as my other obligations allow. I will do you no harm in any manner, and I will grant you one free piece of advice. For this I ask a complete story with as many details as possible. So says Robin Goodfellow. Agreed?"

"Agreed, Mr. The Puck," I replied with a smile.

4
THE OBLIGATORY BACKSTORY

I sat down on a stump across from Mr. The Puck, careful to keep the fire between us. If he noticed my lack of trust, he didn't take offense. He just smiled and settled in, waiting patiently for me to begin. "It was a dark and stormy night," I began solemnly, then laughed. "Just kidding, it was night, but if memory serves there were no clouds, a brilliantly full harvest moon, and it was cold. It wasn't as cold as Daddy thought it was, but it was cold. Daddy hated the cold and anything below seventy was shiver-worthy to him. It was mid-January in Indiana, so pretty much what you would expect, below freezing temperatures with the occasional snowflake falling out of the clear sky.

"I was in what Mama called 'a mood.' Earlier that day I had shot my final ends in the U.S. Nationals archery tournament in Louisville and we were heading home. I placed eleventh overall. You may have noticed the arrows on my pack? Yes? No? Anyway, I shoot Olympic recurve and am darn good at it. I should be. At that time, I had been shooting five to six days a week for three to four hours at a time.

"I was in a mood because, looking back, Daddy was right. I hate that, by the way. I'd shot a lot of arrows and thought I was focused. Daddy had been totally annoying in pointing out that I was not as focused as I thought. I never took him seriously because no one is—um, was—as focused as Daddy. Whether he said he would shoot a hundred serious arrows, or he was going to clean the bathroom, or he was going to get up at a certain time, he always did.

"Anyway, Daddy said I was doing more socializing than shooting and too many people had been telling me how good I was, and not enough people were telling me what I needed to fix. I told him to stop channeling his inner Coach Painter. Daddy took that as a compliment, which I guess is how I meant it.

"Are you a Purdue fan, Mr. The Puck? No? Anyway, Daddy believed Coach Painter was the epitome of a coach. Don't get me wrong, Mr. Puck. Daddy did not care if I was a champion. In fact, he refused to coach me. He believed daddies should be cheerleaders and not coaches. What he did tell me was that I was treating archery like a hobby, and that was okay, but I was going to be competing against people who treated it like a profession, and I shouldn't expect to beat them with my mentality. I was so sure he was wrong.

"Anyway, I was in a mood because I knew I could have shot better. Maybe I couldn't have won, but I could have shot a lot better than I did. I was over crying, well, almost, and was starting to tell myself how I would show Daddy and how I would be so focused and so dedicated that even he would think I was serious. I wanted to tell him so, but I could already hear his response 'That's nice, Munchkin, but actions, not words.'

"Mama and Daddy were talking, and I was mostly not listening while they rehashed the same old conversation about where I would go to college. Mama, who hadn't traveled much because she said she was too afraid younger in life, wanted me to go away. Daddy, who had traveled a lot, was saying I had my whole life to travel and wanted to keep me around for a few more years. I thought the conversation was silly because I was in my second year of high school, but Daddy liked to have a plan for everything, so he and Mama were always talking about what was coming next. It didn't matter to me what conclusion they came to because they'd taught me to make my own decisions and I was going to Oxford if I got in.

"Is this enough detail for you Mr. The Puck?" I asked, starting to cry. "I hope so, because it's at this point in the story where everything changes."

I had to stop for a moment to control my breathing. I'm not certain I will ever be able to remember this part without it tearing me apart. It had already been two years and felt as raw as it did the next day.

"I don't really remember what happened next. I am only going by what I was told and what I could piece together. Apparently, a drunk driver crossed two lanes on the highway and ran into us head on with his car. His car basically exploded, and Mama and Daddy were killed instantly. Our car went off the road and into a small, wooded area where we hit a tree and I was thrown out of the window. I am not sure how I was thrown out, maybe my seatbelt came loose at some point. But Mama and Daddy were still in the car. And it caught fire. I don't really remember any of that. But I guess I had to have been thrown out because I was told Mama and Daddy were found in the car and I was found twenty or so feet away, freezing in the snow.

"I don't remember the ride to the hospital, or even being there. What I was told was I was in a coma for a couple of weeks as I slowly slipped away. One day, a priest from a local college was in praying for me when he thought he noticed a spark or something. He called a colleague who sent a Brother/Doctor to look at me. The Brother/Doctor managed to get me transferred to an experimental medical facility being built in a recently closed building the college had purchased. If that sounds weird to you, well, it did to me as well. They explained to me that a Catholic college in a predominately Catholic city had to be careful with their image. They were not doing anything unethical or immoral, but the world we live in now with its Twitter-based judgement and disbelief in anything scientific had forced them to open anything cutting-edge in a less-than-transparent manner.

"Anyway, um . . . am I saying anyway too often? Mama always said I did. Anyway, I woke up in horrible pain. I mean, everything hurt. I am pretty sure my eyelashes and toenails hurt. I felt like every inch of me was on fire. This went on for what felt like months though the nurses assured me was only a couple of weeks. The nurses would come in twice a day to inject antibiotics and some thick liquid that was supposed to help my bones knit faster. They came in four times a day to give me painkillers and even that wasn't enough. I was in terrible pain and the doctor fretted constantly about my heart rate and blood pressure. All I remember was alternating between pain so bad I screamed and cried, and a feeling of flying and a little relief when the pain meds kicked in.

"But hey, all things must end. Eventually the pain lessened to where I could think and take stock of me and my surroundings. I was not in good shape. I was in a cast from the waist down. Don't ask me how I went to the restroom; it was pretty gross. Also, both arms were in casts and I had on a neck brace and a support for my spine. My vision was very blurry, and I felt like I hadn't showered in months. Other than that, I felt great," I said with a wry smile.

"But back to my story. After what I was told was two weeks, my arm casts were removed, and I could sort of feed myself. I say sort of feed because I had evidently forgotten how to use a spork and I barely had enough energy to lift it in any case. Plus, as an added bonus, my vision was regressing to where everything was basically giant blurs and I had to have the lights turned off in my room because everything was so bright. I still had to be restrained when the bone growth stuff was injected to keep me from thrashing from the pain, but everyone assured me I was very brave and making great progress.

"Eventually, my back and neck braces were removed, and my pain dosages were cut to once a day. It was less than a week after that when they cut off my casts. God, what a relief. I finally got to at least sit in a shower and feel clean again. I was still too weak to walk without help but I could sort of see again, so you know, half full. This was also when they let me know Mama and Daddy didn't make it. I felt horrible because I hadn't even thought about them but between the excruciating pain and the inability to focus on anything else, I am pretty sure they would have forgiven me.

"The rehabilitation started as I slowly got better. The first few days it was just learning to walk again, learning to eat again, take my own showers, that sort of thing. It slowly progressed to yoga, Pilates, and tai chi. As my vision cleared, I was given a Genesis bow, which was similar to the one I had started with as an eight-year old, only this one wasn't pink. Ironically, I had to adjust the bow down to less weight than I used even then. There was no way I could shoot it accurately with so little draw weight, but at least I had a bow in my hand again.

"I also started training in martial arts to build strength and stamina. It was ridiculous, though. I was so weak I could train for maybe five minutes before collapsing in a sweat. When I recovered from that I would shoot ten arrows, badly, and I would be done for an hour. For a girl who was used to shooting three hundred arrows a day, being reduced to barely being able to shoot ten was horrible.

"Surprisingly, as my strength began to return, I started enjoying the martial arts at least as much as the archery. They were a lot like the stuff Daddy used to teach me. There were no forms or katas, or silly bowing or anything like that. They were just moves designed for a little person to do the maximum amount of damage to a big person as quickly as possible. It seemed like an odd way to build my strength, but they assured me that it was for the best. Besides, it was fun.

"I met Brother Damien a few months later. By this time, I was feeling better than I ever had. I mean physically—emotionally I was a kid with no parents, who had already missed a year of school and was tired, scared, and alone. I had put almost three hours straight into exercise, fighting, and stretching and was thinking about shooting when Brother Damien walked in and asked me to come to his office.

"He left before I could follow him, which I thought was amusing. Or rude? Maybe both. See, I didn't know him yet, or where his office was, or even his name, so finding him seemed to be a bit of a stretch. Fortunately, one of my instructors took pity on me and told me where to find him.

"Brother Damien's office was very cluttered, and piles of books and papers were scattered everywhere in no discernible order. He was seated behind what I guessed to be a desk, but it was hard to tell because there wasn't a scrap of desk anywhere to be seen under the clutter. He was older, looked kind, and tired, and a bit apprehensive. What was odd was that he *smelled* apprehensive. I was starting to notice that I could smell stronger moods.

"'Hello, Ms. Malott,' he said in a voice that matched him: a tad high, shaky, and yet kind.

"Daddy always said take the initiative when you weren't sure of what to do. Well, actually, he said, 'Do something, even it's wrong,' but I like my phrasing better. 'Hello, sir, my friends call me Anne with an e. How can I help you?'

"He smiled kindly. 'Hello, Anne with an e. I have been wanting to meet you for a while now. I wanted to wait until you were ready, though. Are you ready?'

"I had no idea what that meant so of course I said 'Sure' because 'sure' was a magic word in our family. It was what Mama had said when Daddy asked her if she wanted to marry him.

"'That's good, Anne. But tell me first, how have things been going?'

"'You mean other than losing my parents, waking up in more casts than clothes, having no idea what I am going to do about my life, school, a place to live, and being an orphan at sixteen?' I said with more amusement than snark. 'Other than that, I guess things are great. How are you doing?'

"Rather than respond directly to my comments, he asked more inane questions and we settled into a surprisingly calm and long conversation. I had a lot of words to get out. I was a

sixteen-year-old girl and I hadn't had anyone to speak to—at?—
for weeks other than nurses and doctors. And they never
wanted to just talk.

"Probably half an hour or so later he asked out of nowhere,
'Do you believe in good and evil, Anne? Do you believe in
monsters? In things that go bump in the night? Magic and
mystery? Things you cannot see? Do you believe in God?'

"'Well, that is tricky. I've always believed in God, but I
suppose I am not too happy with Her right now since She let my
parents die. Good and evil? Sure. I see that every day.
Monsters? Not really. Things that go bump in the night? Other
than me tripping in the dark, no. Daddy always said there was
nothing there when the lights were off that wasn't there when
they were on. Magic? I wish. It would be nice, but no.'

"'Well, all those things are real.' He said it kindly, rather
than trying to talk down to me, which was nice. 'This place is
part of a larger group that works for good and against evil. We
fight monsters and help people who are afraid. I have been
asked to ask you if you would like to join us. Personally, I hope
you say no. I think you are too young and too special to see the
things you would see if you join us.'

"Okay. That little speech ticked me off . . . a lot. 'Look,
Brother Damien. Let me ask you a question. Would you have
said the same thing to a husky sixteen-year-old boy?' When he

hesitated, I went on with even more heat. 'Of course you wouldn't have. Boys are strong and protectors. Girls are around to be protected and to get married and to have kids. You're Catholic, right?' Okay, that was low, but I was on a roll.

"'Let me tell you something: Before the accident I could outshoot Daddy with a bow and outshoot *Mama* with a gun. I was learning to fight from Daddy and, petite or not, I could whup most of the boys in my class. If there were dragons or monsters or things that went bump in the night, I wouldn't be the helpless girl crying to be rescued. I would most likely be having to save the stupid prince since he would be a boy, and that by definition means not usually as smart as a girl.

"'I do not know if I want to join or not, but my age, my hair, or even my boobs are not going to be what makes up my mind, or yours. Now, if we are clear on that you can keep talking; if not, I have arrows to shoot and a life to figure out.'

"'Forgive an old man, Anne,' he said with what a fiction writer might call a wry smile. 'Perhaps I am not as progressive as I like to pretend I am. If you want to start over, then I would like to offer you a chance at a job. You will not be given a position with us, only the chance for one.'

"'And what would I have to do?'

"'Only what you've been doing. Recovering, training hard. I have heard nothing but positive reports about your mental and physical recovery. If I hadn't heard about you in such glowing terms, we would not be having this conversation. Plus, we'd have to switch your medication. So far, we have been focusing on healing you. We do, however, have medication that can make you stronger, make you faster, make your mind clearer. Also, correct your vision.' He smiled, looking at my ugly glasses.

"'You will have to take the medication two to three times a day. You will work until you are exercising twelve hours a day and you will be studying four. You won't need much sleep, the pills will help you with that. You will, however, be sore, tired, and want to quit. If you make it through the next couple of years you will be evaluated for a position.'

"'And if I pass?'

"'You will be a force for good. A light in the darkness,' he said with almost reverence. 'But if you do not, you will not be given a second chance. We have an agreement with the University of Notre Dame. You will be provided with room and board for four years and can pursue whatever vocation you prefer. I am sorry to say that you will most likely be on at least one of the medications for the rest of your life either way.'

"Of course I decided to try, Mr. The Puck. It seemed like the thing to do, you know. I could be a force for good and all. I still thought Brother Damien was putting me on about the monsters and magic and stuff, but at least I had a direction.

"But I tell you, it was the hardest months that I have ever had. My strength came back very quickly and within a couple of months the medication made me everything I was before the accident and much more. I was training with grown men and holding my own. I was pulling a fifty-pound recurve. I was shooting better than I did even at my peak. I studied for hours every day after being beaten mercilessly by sparring partners, stretched, and stabbed with fake knives. I practiced enough with swords to learn at least the basic moves, then stretched some more, lifted weights, and if there was time, I'd do it all over again.

"The coolest thing, Mr. The Puck, was that it seemed I could eat anything and still stay skinny. Well, maybe too skinny, but it was still fun to eat a porterhouse steak and finish it off with a whole apple cobbler pie. I would have preferred to eat more vegetables, but they assured me that with my workload, protein and sugar were my best friends. I even drank their terrible coffee. We'd always cold-pressed ours at home and once you have had good coffee, percolated coffee was nothing more than a disgusting caffeine delivery system.

"Anyway, the last two months of training were by far the strangest. I changed. Really, seemed to change. All of the sudden I was jumping twenty feet in the air with ease. I could no longer spar full out with the men because I was starting to accidentally break them, and they were moving so slowly to me it was like they weren't even trying. Our 'fights' became extreme slow-motion sparring focused entirely on perfect form. I no longer needed to stretch because it seemed that I was permanently flexible. Most of my aches and pains passed before I even knew they were there, and all my old scars had healed. Even the finger I almost cut off a couple years ago on our stupid gate door was now working perfectly."

I reached into my pack and pulled out my baby, showing it to him.

"They gave me my new bow you see here. It pulls like a crossbow and I doubt Jason Momoa could draw it. I can with ease, and it is accurate at least to a couple hundred yards. And now I can *see* that far. In fact, I can see so well that I slept with my eyes covered because the room was never quite dark enough. My hearing is so acute that I can make out individual heartbeats and can even tell whose heartbeat it is, if I know the person. Before I left, I was reading two books a day with more recall than I ever had. My only real challenge was learning to tone down the world around me so I could function. It was like I was me, only more so.

"Anyway, back to my story. I had no idea what tests they were eventually going to give me but I was certain that I was going to pass. Heck, I even took my GED in the middle of all of this so I could be assured of going to the University of Notre Dame if I failed, which I would not. I knew that, but still . . . I was applying to Oxford, but Notre Dame seemed like a nice safety school.

"One morning I was called again to Brother Damien's office. I was pretty excited because I hadn't seen him in a little while, and I was hoping it was time to take the test. 'Well, Anne, it seems you have done all that was asked of you and even more. You have studied more of this library than most of its scholars and I am assured that you are now the epitome of mental and physical health. Are you ready for your last test?'

"He hesitated and looked nervous and unsure. I had never seen him like that. Brother Damien always seemed like he was the smartest and most confident person in the room. It wasn't like he was trying to be seen that way, he really was just the smartest person in the room at any given time and that gave him his confidence. I had been assured on multiple occasions that I was the only one who could fluster him. We never talked about his family, but I thought maybe it was because he never had a daughter or something.

"'You can stop now,' he said slowly. 'Go back to a normal life. Your abilities will return to normal once the medication runs out, and we can switch you to pills that will maintain your health only. If you start the final test there is no turning back. It is quite literally life and death. I would ask that you consider it carefully and take a few days. There is no rush.'

"'What is the final test?'

I was pretty confident I could pass any test. There was no person in the building who could beat me at anything physically and I was positive that I had memorized enough of the books they had given me to get by on any type of scholarly test. The books themselves were an odd blend of physical science, social science, and mythology. I liked the mythology the best because it was a distraction from the oddness my life had become. I read every mythology book they had. I also read all the classics from Adams to Zelazny. There was no way I could go back to a 'normal life' at this point. Everything about me was tuned up to eleven and I enjoyed it. I was never what anyone would call stupid, or slow, but now I was quicker than I ever hoped to be, smarter and stronger too. I could never give that up, Mr. The Puck.

"Brother Damien sighed a sad sigh. 'Do you remember your readings on monsters?'

I nodded but was puzzled. I was going to take a test on monsters? That seemed a tad anticlimactic after all the training I'd been doing.

"'I certainly hope so, because you will be fighting one. You will be facing one alone, in the gym. No weapons of any kind. No armor of any kind. I am sorry, Anne, but you will face this monster alone, and most likely you will not survive the experience. I'm not trying to scare you. I am trying to warn you. Please do not do this. I've already talked to Notre Dame and you are guaranteed admission into the program of your choice in the spring.'

"I smiled at him. 'Scaring me won't work, Brother Damien. I've read all the books about monsters in the library. I mean, the books were great. A lot of them even read like nonfiction. But monsters are not real. Seriously, after all of this the final test is if I am naive enough to believe in monsters? I don't know where you found this guy, or why you think he can beat me when no one else here has even come close, but bring him on.' I smiled. 'I'll beat his butt in under a minute for you.'

"Then, I found out monsters were real. I lost the fight, evidently won some respect, was accepted into the Order, and was sent here to track down and stop a giant bull."

5
BACK TO THE MAIN STORY

"So, there you go, Mr. The Puck," I said sadly.

Thinking about the past never seemed to cheer me up much

unless I was thinking about the archery range. Even that carries a bit of sadness these days.

"Does my story meet with your oh-so-high expectations?"

"It does indeed, young Miss The Munchkin," said the Puck with a wry smile, and surprisingly a hint of sadness. "You have told me much. Much more than you know, and even much more than you guess. The Puck owes you a request and it will be honored. In addition, I will grant you some advice you do not yet know you need.

"People think the shadows are the dark places, and they are. Remember this, Miss The Munchkin. Remember it well and consider it often: The light breeds many shadows, and not all shadows are dark and not all light is bright. Rather, they are both merely grays on the continuum of light and dark. Ponder that often in your many journeys."

Then he smiled and pointed to a spot behind me. "While you are pondering, I will ask you to step into the tree you see behind you. It will allow you passage to the land of the Bull. I cannot get you to the Bull directly. The most the Puck can do for now is to get you into his realm. Even I do not know his exact location, or where you will arrive, for both are tied to you, and not to me. At best, you will arrive in his castle. However"—he smiled—"as we both know, 'the best' rarely happens, so I assume you will be some days' journey from where you need to be. Also, consider that time passes differently where you will be going, so I also do not know when you will return, if, of course, you do return. Occasionally decades pass, but most often it is more a matter of a few hours depending upon, of course, how long you are there.

"I warn you to be very careful as the realm of the Bull is not a friendly place," he said sternly. "In fact, it will most assuredly be very inhospitable to you, for you come to slay the ruler of the realm. As your thoughts guide your journey, I can only guess that you will start in a less-than-peaceful place. Those who seek blood often find it. I bid you good day."

"Wait!" I cried. "How will I return? If time passes differently there, then how do I know how much time I have to find the bull and stop this before it is too late? What other advice can you give me?"

"Return?" Mr. The Puck smiled. "I doubt seriously that you will. You are on a questing in a land of which you have no knowledge, to slay a creature that legend says cannot die. No, young Miss The Munchkin, sadly I believe this is goodbye for us.

"I will grant you this, though, for the wonderful tale you told me. I will spread rumor among the court that a warrior has come to slay the bull and will be arriving within two weeks."

"Two weeks?" I stammered. "I have to find a ruler in a land that I do not know, starting from possibly anywhere, going somewhere, to stop a guy you just mentioned can't be stopped? All within two weeks? What if I start at the other end of this realm? Are you crazy? That is nowhere near enough time. And what 'realm' am I going to anyway? And what did you mean by he can't be killed?"

The Puck laughed again. He does that a lot. "Call the realm 'Faerie,' for that is close enough for your purposes. All realms seem to be Faerie to mortals. As to your second question, do you really believe the bull will have nothing better to do than to wait on a young girl's wishes? He will be honor-bound to answer your challenge. But he cannot wait forever. Any longer than two weeks and he will rightfully consider this to be a fool's quest. In truth, he will consider it to be so in any case, but he will wait a short time, if only to affirm to his followers he has no fear of mortal challengers. And he truly does have no fear of you, or any mortal. It has been said that he is one of the great fighters in the lands.

"As for returning to this realm, if you wish to make another bargain with the Puck, well, I can try to bring you home. I wish very little in exchange. You let me into the Keep of the Light Bringers when you return, and I will come once when called. I cannot guarantee I can aid when called, but the Puck will do his best when, and if he arrives."

"Thank you, but no, Mr. The Puck. I have promised never to

allow passage to another, or even reveal the location, though I am pretty sure it is well known to a lot of people. If Munchkin was foresworn in this, how could you trust her word to you? I'll get this done within two weeks, and then find my own way back."

I turned and looked at the tree. It was old and gnarly. I can't really explain it, but somehow the tree did not look friendly. It looked as if it didn't like me. Oh, yeah, and it had not been there five minutes ago. Maybe I should have led with that. Anyway, there was just enough of an opening for someone my size to squeeze through if I held my go-bag beside me and turned sideways.

"One last question, Mr. The Puck. Will my belongings go with me?" But when I turned, he was gone. I turned back and entered the tree, hoping that I would not see some version of me where I would have to cut off its head, and squeezed in.

6
THE LAND OF THE BULL

The inside of the tree was much larger than the outside, which was way cool! It was at least ten feet wide and stretched far enough into the distance that I couldn't see its end. Mostly though, after the novelty wore off, it was just dull and repetitive. While there seemed to be spiderwebs everywhere I didn't see a spider, or insect, or really anything at all that was alive, other than moss. A faint fog was omnipresent but never got higher than my knees. Basically, it was a boring, uneventful couple hundred yards or so until I saw an opening in the distance. That was when it struck me just how different things had become. I had just walked a "boring and uneventful" distance through a tree that was not large enough for me to walk ten paces around it.

Oh, well, Mama said there'd be days like this.

As I stepped outside of the tree, the strangeness of all this hit me even harder. It was like I was in a fantasy novel or something. Okay, I was still in the woods, but it was definitely different woods than I had been in five minutes ago. The trees were taller and old enough that they blanketed the sky, and there was almost no growth on the ground. I was guessing it was still close to the middle of the night but there was no way to be sure as I could not see past the canopy of leaves a hundred feet up or so.

I could, however, hear a lot of laughter only a couple

hundred yards away and saw the glow of a fire pit. The laughter itself was odd and sounded more animal than human.

This should be interesting, I thought as I started to make my way toward the fire.

But I only made it about twenty steps when I passed a tree, was grabbed, had a knife placed to my throat, and felt a beefy arm wrap around my chest. Okay, well, my throat wasn't instantly cut in spite of my lack of caution so I might as well see how this played out.

I took a deep breath as if to yell and leaned back into my attacker but hesitated long enough for him (it? her?) to seize back the initiative.

"Quiet!" he yell-whispered.

Definitely a he.

"I don't know what you're doing sneaking around at night but if you make too much noise then I'll have to share. And I think we both'd rather that didn't happen. Now wouldn't we?"

Well. I had several of my answers. Definitely male. Definitely not friendly. Definitely with the group ahead. And, oh yeah, stupid. Since I was leaning back anyway, I simply raised my foot and stomped on his hard enough to break it. One hand went up to make sure my throat was not cut and the other down to grab him and squeeze where no male likes a good, hard squeeze. He started to scream, and since I was mostly free at that point, I spun around with a left elbow to break his jaw and keep him quiet.

Only, that is where this whole thing got even weirder. I didn't break his jaw. Instead, I broke a tusk and man oh man, did that hurt my elbow. Fortunately, it also seemed to stun him, so I kicked him where I'd just finished squeezing. As he fell to both knees, I grabbed the back of his head and kneed him in the face, hard enough to knock him out even if it didn't slam his head into the tree behind him. Which it did. Stupid jerk. Attacking an innocent young girl. Anyway, he was not a current threat, so I slid behind the tree to see if anyone came running to his rescue.

Apparently, we weren't that loud because the noise at the fire never changed. Yay! I found some rope on him and tied him securely after removing his other two knives and a short sword. Then I gagged him as best I could. While doing so I just happened to notice he was a pig. I mean, like literally a pig. He was dressed in peasant clothes, talked, and stood on two legs, but other than that he looked just like a giant boar whose snout was a little shorter than normal. Guess I really wasn't in Illinois anymore. He also had on a cap that appeared to be made of steel so either I wasn't in Faerie, or all the myths were wrong, and I had read all those mythology books for nothing. His pockets yielded a couple of silver coins and nothing else.

Back to the matter at hand. I needed information on where to find the Bull King, or whatever he was called. I had a tied-up boar at my feet and presumably more of them around the fire up ahead. I doubted they'd be happy I decked their friend but, you never know, maybe he had been on guard duty because none of the other pigs liked him. He certainly didn't seem that likeable to me. Regardless, I was going to be a lot more cautious this time, so I circled the camp slowly to see if there were any more sentries. There weren't, but now I had a much better idea of what I was dealing with. There were three more pigs drinking by the fire and one much larger one resting by a tree a couple of feet away.

Lying next to the larger pig and trussed up like a Christmas ham (joke intended), appeared to be a smaller man—say, my height. The pigs were joking about how much money the man had on him and how good he was going to (gak!) taste as stew once they got around to making some. Well, I was on a mission to save kids, but it seemed as if I was going to have to get involved with saving an adult, too. I didn't like the odds, but it wasn't as if I could just let this poor guy get eaten.

"Hello, boys," I said, coming out of the shadows and positioning myself so the three smaller boars (three little pigs?) were between me and the giant one. "Sorry to ruin your good time but it appears I don't have a much of a choice. You see, I am with this super-secret organization that helps protect the innocent. I'm relatively new at it, but I am pretty certain part of helping people is keeping them from getting eaten by pigs. Now, I'm not big on trouble. You know, as the great man once said, 'Don't start nothin', won't be nothin', so just let me have the man you have tied up over there and I'll be on my merry."

I really didn't think my little speech would help all that much other than either (1) prove how innocent I am and therefore harmless or (b) enrage them so they'd be off balance.

The pigs stared at each other for about a half second before leaping up and grabbing clubs. At least they chose clubs instead of swords. It appeared they went with the "She's harmless, let's just knock her out option." Excellent. Then they charged me without even proper spacing between them which was just sad. They had as much chance of hitting each other as they did of hitting me.

Anyway, the one in the middle raised his club as high as he possibly could and slammed it down at my head. It surely would have killed me had it not been so slow, telegraphed, and just plain embarrassing. Since I didn't feel like being squashed like a grape, I shifted slightly to the left and let his swing throw him totally off balance. His friend to the right went with an Aaron Judge swing to my head which made for a truly fun one, two. I ducked his swing and let him hit his buddy—who just missed my head—solidly in the ribs (told you so!). Then, I kicked him in the little piggies as hard as I could. I know that seems to be my go-to move, but when you are half the mass of the people you usually fight, such a glaring weakness is a handy target. Now I had one down on his knees, one with broken ribs, and a third who took a few steps back and was looking confused that the helpless little girl was kicking serious pig butt.

"This can end now," I said as calmly as possible. I had an adrenaline rush from the fight, so I knew my voice was a bit shaky, but I think it came out okay. "Just let me have the dude tied up over there and we can be on our way."

He pondered that for a second, but the giant pig by the fire cleared his throat and nodded at me to let me know he expected him to fight, so this was going to happen.

"You're dead, little human," he grunted while dropping his club and drawing a thick dagger. "I am going to carve you up and put you into the stew."

"Uh-huh," I said cleverly while taking a step back and to the left. He had started tossing his knife from hand to hand and I wanted his backside to the fire. "Stop that," I said, stomping my foot. "It's embarrassing."

"Huh?" he replied, looking at me with confused piggy eyes.

"Stop tossing your knife back and forth. You're going to drop it. Act like a man, er, pig, whatever. Take this seriously," I said, hoping he was as stupid as he looked.

He was. He looked down at his knife and I quickly took a half step forward and kicked him in the chest, and directly into the fire. He scrambled in it for a couple of seconds and then ran off, stumbling and trying to get his burning pants off. Honestly, he sort of smelled like bacon. Okay, delicious—but gross. I was going to be conflicted for a while if I survived.

"That was embarrassing," said the giant while climbing to his feet.

Crap! He must be seven feet tall and not in a skinny way. Well, I hoped I was either faster or more skilled than he was. If he was as fast and skilled as me then I was dead. I mean, I'm strong and fast, like really strong and really fast, but I seriously doubted I was as strong as a giant boar.

"I want you to know these are not my regular crew," he rumbled in a voice I could almost feel. "They suffered a 'mishap' recently and I had to make do." He paused for a second to crack his pig knuckles. "Tell you what. Why don't you join me? It seems I have a few positions that recently opened."

"That's really flattering," I said in all insincerity, while walking to my go-bag and grabbing my bow, "but there are a couple of things we should discuss first. One, a girl working for a boss who is a big pig is almost too trite to be funny, and b, I am not really the criminal type. And three, that knife you have behind your back is not nearly as concealed as you think it is. You really are too big for that type of subtlety. Tell you what. Counteroffer? You take what's left of your, um, people? Leave me the guy you have trussed up and I don't see if I can make some record-breaking chops out of you." Okay, I was bluffing. No way I was going to eat a sentient being. But I was really going for just upsetting him as much as possible. Very few people can fight when they are angry.

It seemed to work. He let out a deep growl and threw the knife he had "hidden" behind his back straight at my head. Since I didn't feel like taking a knife to the head, I ducked to the left and nocked an arrow. "Last chance, big piggy, don't make me hurt you. That armor of yours won't stop these arrows." I guess he thought I was bluffing because he took a step my way. "Not another step," I warned. He continued toward me and seemed genuinely surprised when I shot him in the heart. I'm not sure what he expected. I did say not to take another step. He managed to take one more before crashing to his knees, and then face down in the dirt.

The arrow had gone almost all the way through him, so I removed it and cleaned it off, which smelled way better than I wanted to admit to myself. Then I approached the man tied up by the fire. "Well, now, what do I do with you? For the moment

we are going to assume you are an innocent victim in all of this.
Tell me first," I asked while carefully cutting off the gag, "who
you are and how did you get yourself in this predicament?"

I dragged him back a few feet and sat him up against a
nearby tree while he worked his jaw enough to be able to talk.
They had gagged him very tightly. Then I studied him and
waited. He was a very dark man, and perhaps a shade under
five feet tall. He seemed thin and wiry, but it was hard to tell
while he was bundled up so tightly. He looked maybe fifty years
old but honestly, anyone over thirty is so old it's hard to tell fifty
from seventy. His eyes were dark as coal and his hair was wiry
and cut close to his head.

"Let's start with your name, sir."

"Water, if you please, ma'am," he croaked. "Wearing a gag for
a couple of days is thirsty work. Perhaps something stronger, if
you have it? I thought I saw a skin of wine being passed around
earlier."

"Let's start with this," I said, fetching a cup of water so he
could take some sips. "I still haven't decided exactly what I am
going to do with you. Keeping you from being eaten is one thing,
trusting you is quite another."

"Very well," he said after a few sips. His voice was deep and
rich. I found myself wanting to hear him sing. "My name is
Stagger Lee."

I threw the cup aside in disgust. Anyone who has ever listened to blues music knew his tale, and Daddy listened to a lot of blues. That means I had to listen to them as well. Stagger Lee was, best case, a scoundrel. And that was the best case.

"Well then, Mr. Lee, I am terribly sorry to have rescued you. I am not in the habit of making friends with pimps, murderers, gang members, and whatever else you may be. I am sure you can free yourself in time."

With that, I turned my back on him and began scouring the camp for useful items and fixing the arrowhead so it would be useful later. I only had twenty shafts and forty heads, and I had no idea how long I was going to be on this quest.

"Oh, and by the way, where is your hat?"

"Ah," he said sadly. "It seems you've heard the tale. Well, my young savior, don't you be believing all the tales and wild stories you've heard about old Stagger. How about this? How about I tell you my tale and you make up your own mind about me?"

I shushed him and listened as carefully as I could. The other pigs were gone for now, so it appeared we had a little time at least. So, I made a "Get on with it" motion with my hands.

7

THE TRUE-ISH STORY OF STAGGER LEE

"Why don't you be untying me, little girl? My story would be easier to tell if I wasn't cramping up so much," he asked hopefully and with the slightest bit of a whine.

I hate whiners.

"Why don't you be telling me your story while I get some food on and you stop your whining. I hate whiners," I said while examining the stewpot. "Oh, start with what is cooking."

"Just vegetables so far. We're good. I think that part about cooking me was mostly bluff," he said, smiling. "But okay, so my tale. I grew up in a rougher part of NOLA. There wasn't any honest work, so I gravitated toward hustling, gambling, that sort of thing. You know—"

"Pimping?" I asked wryly while rummaging through the pigs' coin purses. I wasn't familiar with the local currency, but it seemed like they had a heck of a lot of coins.

"Nope," he replied in an offended tone. "That was a downright dirty lie. I had me a good woman or two that I hung with. Sometimes they'd give me money and I'd protect them or something if things were bad, but it wasn't no formal arrangement or nothing."

"Uh-huh," I said in a tone of total disbelief. "Sounds like you were truly a Knight Protector for fair maidens. I get it. Enjoy your ropes. I'm going to eat some stew and then I am out of here."

I started in the on the stew and it was truly delicious. There were flavors that I didn't even know existed. One of those pigs could definitely cook.

"Wait!" he cried with almost the right amount of fear. I wanted him a lot more scared or a lot more contrite before deciding what to do with him. Right now, the odds of me freeing him were not in his favor.

"Look, girl, it was a different time. I'm not proud of it, and I put all that behind me." He paused and seemed a little sad while thinking.

Not so sad that I was believing him but maybe, just maybe, it was a start.

"I met a girl, see. She was as beautiful and loving as a man could want. Her name was Maybellene. Maybe she wasn't the truest woman in the world, but she was a good woman. We started to have a really good thing and I was leaving some of my more colorful past behind me. No more strange women. There was less drinking and other things, and more hustling with the crew. I pretty much done quit the robbery and stuff and was making my money gamblin'. Turns out when you ain't drinkin' so much, and everyone else is, gamblin' got a lot easier.

"So anyway, one night I was shooting dice in the back of an alley with a couple of fellows from a social club I was runnin' with, a couple of people I didn't know so well, and a no-good scoundrel named Billy Lyon. Now Billy and I never liked each other much and I knew I should probably walk away but I had made a few passes in a row and things were goin' well."

He paused and shook his head. It looked for all the world like he was at a loss for words and I thought the story was ending until he suddenly spoke again in a sad and low voice. The kind of voice that again made me wish I could hear him sing.

"Then I took a quick break. I needed to get rid of a couple beers I'd been drinkin' earlier and Billy took the dice. But he sure seemed eager to get them back to me when I came back. At the time, I took it for him just wanting to try to take advantage of my streak, but he bet against me and raised the stakes hard. Now I ain't never been no fool so I put the dice down and told them all I'd see them another day. That's when things started to get ugly. Even the boys I usually run with weren't happy with me leaving so far ahead so I got out of there quick as quick. I didn't need that kind of trouble and I was up pretty fair anyway."

He stopped again to collect his thoughts and I gave him a few sips of water to help him finish his tale.

"It was only a few blocks down the street when I noticed that I didn't have my Stetson. Now I loved that hat, it being a gift from my lady and all, so I decided right then and there I was going back and gettin' that hat back no matter what. If I'd a been thinkin' clearer, I would a waited 'til the next day. But that hat meant a lot to me and Billy Lyons meant a whole lot to me in a whole different direction. So, when I walked back into the alley it was with the gun I usually carry in the back of my pants in my hand.

"There was only Billy Lyons and the guys I didn't know left in the alley. Billy was wearin' my hat, which pissed me off something fierce. I told Billy to just give me the hat an' everything'd be fine. He didn't, though. He called me a coward hidin' behind a gun and said there were three of them and one of me and I couldn't get them all. I figured he was correct on that and if I gave them the chance, I was dead. So, I shot him square in the chest and told the others to git. After they did, I took my hat and headed for home."

There were tears in his eyes now.

"That hat cost me more than I ever knew. I went up the river for a spell. When I got back, I found that I had lost my hat, my woman, and everythin' I'd ever owned. I had nothin' and no reason. I went back to drinkin' and robbin' and generally not caring about anything until I was caught and sent back to prison. I thought I'd die there and didn't much care, but one day I just woke up here feelin' younger than I had in years and wonderin' where all this freedom and space came from.

"I've spent the last few months here lookin' for my hat and tryin' to get the lay of the land. Then I ran into some pigs who had no knowledge of how to play dice. I thought it was my duty to teach 'em and next thing you know, I went from winnin' a few coins to bein' trussed up in a sack and figurin' I was going to be a meal."

"Okay," I said without much pity for his predicament. "I don't have much pity for your predicament. It seems to me like tied up is pretty much how you belong." I pretended to think about it while he protested and whined about life being unfair. "I'll tell you what," I said after a few minutes of incessant whining, "why don't you tell me everything that you know about this place, where I can find the King Bull or whatever he is called, and anything else you think I might find useful and I might find it in my heart to free you. The pigs I didn't kill seemed to have wandered off so you might be free for a while. I might even feel kind enough to leave you some supplies."

"Fair deal," he said, leaping at the chance to exchange

freedom for the stewpot. "Well, let's see. I assume you want to kill the Bull King? That's what I always heard him called, in any case." He looked at me with an air of expectation. I nodded and he continued. "I've heard rumors some warrior was gunnin' for him. Never thought it would be a girl warrior, though."

At my less than amused look he started talking again, very quickly. "Well, that makes it much more difficult. You see, this land seems to give you the opposite of what you want. It's almost like everythin' is set up to be hard. Now I'll be honest and tell you I don't know much, and what I do know is stuff I've picked up listenin' in the small towns I've visited. So, I don't know the truth to all of it. I guess that is the first thing I'd tell you. When the sun comes up, walk toward it. Walk a day or so and you'll find yourself in a small hamlet. It's on your way anyway because everythin' I've heard is your man, er, bull, lives in a castle surrounded by a giant maze far to the east. That's all I've heard. I swear it."

"That's not really a lot of information," I said.

It's a good thing this guy shot dice instead of playing poker because his face was an open book. I finished packing up all the supplies that I thought I'd need. Or at least, all the supplies I could scavenge.

"You may have earned me maybe leaving you some food, but I think you haven't earned enough trust for me to actually let you go. I guess I could leave you with a knife stuck in the ground or something so you can free yourself. Maybe you can even get free before the pigs come back. So long," I said, slinging my go-bag onto my back and positioning it so it wouldn't be too cumbersome in a surprise fight.

"Wait!" he cried, and I hid a smile from him. I was bluffing about leaving. I needed him good and scared so that he wouldn't try any lies or half-truths. "I didn't mention the rest because I didn't know for sure it was true and I thought— Well, I thought if you knew just how impossible this quest of yours is, you'd just kill me and be done with it." He paused. "After you get to the town you have to pass through the Centaur Wood. The centaurs don't like people and don't tolerate no one in their woods. And the maze? Well, that speaks for itself."

"Fine. I am grabbing a couple hours' sleep. I hate to waste the time, but I've been up for hours, and frankly, all of this," I said, pointing around, "has been a little hard on my nerves. I need a couple hours to recharge. You are a free man in the morning. I will be heading east. I would rather you head another direction. Nothing personal, I just don't trust you."

8

CAUGHT IN A LOOP

After not enough sleep, I woke up surprisingly refreshed, cut Stagger Lee loose, and left without a goodbye. He looked at me for a moment as if he wanted to say something but decided against it. I thought that was odd as he was a talkative little guy, but I didn't pay it much attention as I headed east through the woods, looking for random hamlets and villages.

I didn't immediately find either, but what I did find was amazing. After about an hour of walking, the trees suddenly ended, and I saw rolling grasslands that stretched farther than even my enhanced vision could see. It was beautiful in a way I have never seen, or even imagined. Everything should be described in CAPITAL LETTERS. The grass waving gently in the breeze was GREEN. The sky was BLUE, and the clouds were . . .. Well, you get it. Everything was just *more*. Even the air seemed to cleanse my lungs with each breath.

I wondered briefly if my world was like this before all the

pollution, but I doubted it. As a family, we had visited many state parks and woodlands on holidays. All of them had been beautiful and clean and full of nature, but none of them could live up to this. Even the temperature seemed perfect. Not too hot, not too cold, just right. I felt a tension I didn't even know I had slip away.

Of course, that made me sad because I remembered Daddy always telling me that my life was not hard, we were very lucky and needed to remember that, even in the worst of times. I missed my parents. Then, of course, I remembered Daddy saying to stop "pissing and moaning" about things I can't control and to keep pushing on the things I can. I stepped into the plains with that thought and within a mile or so was back in a pleasant mood. It was just too beautiful for any mood other than peaceful.

Within fifteen miles (give or take) my mood was starting to slip in spite of the peace. It was not that anything had happened, or even that I thought anything bad could happen. I hadn't seen anything more threatening than small game and birds. I also had not seen any sign of civilization. But the sun was starting to set, and I figured it was time to secure a campsite and settle in for the night before dark. I could see in close to zero light, but if *Don't Starve Together* had taught me anything, it was the value of a campfire at night to keep the monsters and things you cannot see away. It also taught me that just because you wanted a campsite, that did not mean you had the wood for one, or even a suitable shelter space.

So, with every place looking like every other place, every place was equally good. With that cheery thought, I went to sleep looking up at a beautiful sky with so many stars it almost seemed as if the sky had just little spots of darkness rather than little spots of light.

I fell into a deep and wondrously peaceful, if too short sleep.

***

After not enough sleep, I woke up surprisingly refreshed, cut Stagger Lee loose, and left without a goodbye. He looked at me for a moment as if he wanted to say something but decided against it. I thought that was odd as he was a talkative little guy, but I didn't pay it much attention as I headed east through the woods, looking for random hamlets and villages.

I didn't immediately find either, but what I did find was amazing. After about an hour of walking the trees suddenly ended, and I saw rolling grasslands that stretched farther than even my enhanced vision could see. It was beautiful in a way I have never seen, or even imagined. Everything should be described in CAPITAL LETTERS. The grass waving gently in the breeze was GREEN. The sky was BLUE, and the clouds were . . .. Well, you get it. Everything was just *more*. Even the air seemed to cleanse my lungs with each breath.

I wondered briefly if my world was like this before all the pollution, but I doubted it. As a family, we had visited many state parks and woodlands on holidays. All of them had been beautiful and clean and full of nature, but none of them could live up to this. Even the temperature seemed perfect. Not too hot, not too cold, just right. I felt a tension I didn't even know I had slip away.

Of course, that made me sad because I remembered Daddy always telling me that my life was not hard, we were very lucky and needed to remember that, even in the worst of times. I missed my parents. Then, of course, I remembered Daddy saying to stop "pissing and moaning" about things I can't control and to keep pushing on the things I can. I stepped into the plains with that thought and within a mile or so was back in a pleasant mood. It was just too beautiful for any mood other than peaceful.

Within fifteen miles (give or take) my mood was starting to slip in spite of the peace. It was not that anything had happened, or even that I thought anything bad could happen. I hadn't seen anything more threatening than small game and birds. I also had not seen any sign of civilization. But the sun was starting to set, and I figured it was time to secure a campsite and settle in for the night before dark. I could see in close to zero light, but if *Don't Starve Together* had taught me anything, it was the value of a campfire at night to keep the monsters and things you cannot see away. It also taught me that just because you wanted a campsite, that did not mean you had the wood for one, or even a suitable shelter space.

So, with every place looking like every other place, every place was equally good. With that cheery thought, I went to sleep looking up at a beautiful sky with so many stars it almost seemed as if the sky had just little spots of darkness rather than little spots of light.

I fell into a deep and wondrously peaceful, if too short sleep.

***

After not enough sleep I woke up surprisingly refreshed, cut Stagger Lee loose, and left without a goodbye.

Well, this is officially weird in a totally sucky way, I thought. This all seemed very *deja vu* to me. With that cheery thought, I turned around and went back to the campfire.

"Hey, Stagger, ever feel like you're having *deja vu*?"

"Can't rightly say that I have. Is that anything like *maque choux*? I haven't had me any good *maque choux* since I got here."

"What? You eat mock shoes? I've been hungry before but never hungry enough to eat my shoes. I guess I have been lucky."

"Not shoe, girl, *choux, maque choux.*" He smiled. "You cook onions and peppers and garlic and corn and tomatoes until they're really thick. Then add cream until it all looks like it'll melt in your mouth. Mama always added bacon drippings and hot sauce. It's so good you can eat it every day and so hot you get mad at yourself just for eatin' it. Now, some people make it sweet like dessert, but hot is the way to go," he said with reverence. "Why? You got any?"

"Sorry, Stagger. I said *déjà vu.* It's sort of a feeling like you've done the same thing before, only you cannot quite remember when or where."

"Oh, that." He frowned. "That's probably just old Mobius messin' with you. He likes to do that sometimes with new people. Just don't worry about it. He'll get bored in time and move on to someone else. It's not like you really lose anything because you always end up right back where you started no matter where you go or what you do. I think I lost a few weeks when I first got here doing that. Hard to say, though. Could've been a few months or years. You know when everything just starts over, it's hard to tell how many times it just started over."

"That is totally unacceptable. I can't just keep reliving the same day—uh, days?—over and over again here. I have a mission to get done and it has to get done soon."

"Well," he replied thoughtfully. Or maybe his head just

itched because he was scratching it kind of hard. "Do you know Ariadne? She could help you. She's terribly hard to find, though. Ain't no one I know but her could get old Mobius to stop. Without her you'll be stuck until he gets bored."

"I've never had the pleasure," I said with what patience I had left. "Where can I find her?"

"Well." He scratched his head even harder. I was starting to worry about fleas. "You can't. I think she took off or something. Word is she's hiding out with some secret group or something."

"How do you know this? Who told you? I have to find her! Dang it! Kids are going to die, and I am going to be stuck here forever without her help," I cried, near tears. It happens. Get over it.

"I've never met her or anyone who has. That's just the word. I guess she was always one for puzzles or something. Word is she just took off because too many folks were going to her asking for stuff or something. Word is she just left a note and said only the one who could figure it out was worth talkin' to. The story is kinda famous around here. Everyone knows about it." He hesitated. "Now that's just weird. I mean everyone knows about it, but I'm not sure I did until you asked me. This place is sure odd sometimes."

"Awesome," I said, thinking he was (a) right about the place being weird, and (2) an exasperating tour guide. "Where can I find the note?"

"I've never seen it."

"Do you know what it said?"

"Oh, yeah. Now that you mention it, I do. I'm not sure I knew before you mentioned it, but now? Well, now I do."

"And?"

"And what?"

"WHAT DOES THE FREAKING NOTE SAY?"

9
ARIADNE'S RIDDLES

"Oh, that." He struck a pose that was supposed to make him look like an orator or something before responding. "'Only she who *uncovers a cabal* can find me.' That don't make no sense to me. I ain't seen no cables around here anywhere. I guess that's what it means. Find the buried cable."

"One question," I said, trying to think this through.

"Only one?" he replied with a friendly smile. "You ain't stopped asking questions since I met you, girl."

"Whatever. Why did you put the emphasis on the words *uncovers a cabal*?"

"I don't rightly know. I guess that's just how I remembered it."

"Okay. Thanks," I said because I was trying to remember my manners.

"You're welcome, little girl. I reckon I'm headin' out now. I want to get far away from the rest of the boars as I can."

"See you," I replied absently. "Wait! Rest of the boars? And where is the one I killed?" But he was gone. *Idiot men.*

Okay, Munchkin. Let's figure this out. Evidently more boars were around here, and once the ones I didn't kill find the group I met they might get uppity and come back to even the score. I needed to be gone by then.

This riddle was evidently person-specific since it said "she." Let's start with that. It has to be something that I can solve, but almost certainly something that Ariadne didn't want anyone to solve easily, so it was probably a riddle within a riddle.

Well, let's see. I walked for a day and ended up back where I started. I didn't see any groups of people at all. The only group I did find were the boars and not only do I think they were not really a cabal, I didn't actually uncover them. So that wasn't it. So, what's next? Uncover. Solve? Yeah. That felt right. What am I solving here? Stagger emphasized *uncovers a cabal* when he spoke. Let's start there.

Uncovers a cabal. What kind of anagram would that make?

And why wasn't anagram an anagram? Stop it, and think, girl. Okay. Vascular beacon? That's weird. I suppose I could look for a spotlight tonight but that didn't feel right. Abacas can lover? Nah. That's just too weird. Accruals be nova? Mama was an accountant and she said weird stuff like that all the time when she was trying to be funny, but I didn't see how that could help me. Casual bra coven? Sounds like a group I'd like to join but not particularly helpful. Aaargh! Dang it, Munchkin. Think it through. A riddle within a riddle.

An hour later I was pretty certain I had it. *Caverna sub laco.* Cave under a lake. It was designed for me—years of Catholic school Latin, darn near impossible to figure out and, ultimately, really satisfying. When I had it, I knew I had it. Now, to find a lake, or a pond.

I had a little while until dark and no idea where to find water. I chose the way that made the most sense to me and walked the opposite direction of where I went the first time. That actually didn't make sense, of course, since a Mobious loop would always just keep bringing me back. But I was playing by a whole new set of rules now that, evidently, I was in Faerie. I just hoped maybe this spot, being where I came into this world, was the hopping on and off point. Which again made no sense since a Mobious loop had neither of those. But hey, a girl's gotta try.

Twenty minutes later, I was at the shore of what appeared to me to be a person-made, two-acre pond. It looked perfectly round and had a beach two feet around it. At the cardinal points were large, round boulders surrounded by smaller boulders, again at cardinal points. The water was almost crystal clear, and I could see at least twenty feet down to the bottom.

The issue: I *could* see almost twenty feet down to the bottom. And I didn't see any caves. In fact, I walked all around the pond and didn't see anything but a smooth lake bottom. That meant if I was right about the anagram, the cave would have to be smack in the middle somewhere, and I was going in for an exploratory swim.

The good news was the symmetry of the pond meant that the cave almost had to be in the center. The bad news was the center of the pond looked to be a full twenty feet deep. That was not a hard dive by any means, but I felt the water and it was cold. I mean, really cold. Darn cold. Stupid cold. How the heck was it so cold? I couldn't see how it wasn't covered in ice.

With that cheery thought I built a small fire and made sure it would burn for a while without spreading. I didn't think I could last more than ten minutes in that water without becoming a Munchkincicle, and I wanted to be as fresh as possible before making the attempt. I also really wanted to wait for full daylight so I could see a lot better, but I wasn't sure if I'd lost zero, or three days to Mobius, so I needed to push as hard as I could.

Pushing hard was one thing. Not preparing was another. No sense dying to save an hour. First, I threw a couple of small rocks and twigs in the pond. They didn't dissolve or instantly freeze over or anything, so I had that going for me. Second, the pond was completely empty of life so far as I could see, so I was probably not going to be fighting pond monsters. Third, the cold and the wet. The really cold and wet. Oh, well, no help for it, at least I had a fire to come back to.

I stripped down to my Typhon Skin (Trademark) body suit. It wasn't as good as having all my clothes but was WAY better than nothing. It hugged the body like silk but could stop most knife slashes (probably not hard thrusts, though I hadn't checked that thoroughly) and even kept low velocity bullets from penetrating—although they still hurt like the dickens unless they hit the ballast plate directly. The suit had slit pockets for three thin knives, one on each leg and one on my left sleeve. That was not great, but better than nothing. The knives were polymer so I could slip through most security screenings and I wasn't worried about rust. I put the rest of my gear in my travel bag, climbed a tree about thirty feet up, and camouflaged them as best I could. If I survived this little swim, I wanted to make sure I had gear for the rest of the trip. The Typhon Skin was handy but did not retain heat. It would also certainly draw entirely too much male attention. Boys are stupid.

I looked around one last time, did not see any imminent danger, or any houses on the left, so I waded in a few feet and then dove. No sense getting partially frozen when the cold was going to happen. Daddy said it was like death, taxes, and Purdue basketball suffering a major injury before the tournament. Some things were inevitable.

Um . . . I seriously underestimated the cold of the water. COLD did not begin to describe it. I almost instantly froze darn near solid. My muscles bunched up and I involuntarily gasped, causing the icy water to flood into my lungs. Fortunately, I was still only fifteen feet out, not quite deeper than head height, when I managed to stand up. It took everything I had to get my body moving back toward shore. I was panicked the entire time as it was a very slow race between freezing to death and wading back to shore. Since I am writing this to you it is obvious which one won. But it was close. I barely had the energy to crawl to my fire when I reached shore. I just puked up ice water, and stew, and energy bars, and something I'm certain I had eaten weeks ago, curled into a ball and waited for the fire to warm me enough to start moving again.

Thirty minutes or so later I was mostly dry—except for my hair which was going to be a problem for another hour or so—

and completely without a plan. Well, not really. I had a plan, but it was not a good one. If I was wrong about there being a cave in the middle of the lake, then I was dead. If I was right, I was still most likely dead. So, you know, not a great plan. But I figured Ariadne really did not want to be found unless the finder really wanted to find her, so near death was a given. I was starting to not like that bitch.

I carried two logs that seemed big enough to support my weight to the shore and lashed them together with some paracord I keep in my go-bag. I also grabbed one of the smaller boulders, say a hundred pounds or so, and set it by the logs. It was not great having to climb the tree again, but what are you going to do?

Also, if you are ever going anywhere more than five minutes from civilization, carry a lot of paracord. My paracord is 275 since I weigh in at around one hundred and fifty even carrying 50 pounds in my go-bag. It is a great compromise between strength and the ability to hold on to it. That stuff is as useful as duct tape, which I also always carried. Take that, Daddy! He always said I would have a permanent hunch because even when I was back in grade school, I carried a bag he laughingly said would get me through at least the first year of a zombie apocalypse. I haven't seen one of those yet but I'm sure at some point I will. That is just how my life works these days.

Anyway, I tied a couple loops around the rock and fastened a handhold, put it on my modified raft, pushed it all into the pond, climbed on, and paddled with a flat piece of bark out to what I thought was about the exact middle of the pond. Now came the fun part. Or, I should say, the not-fun part where I was most likely going to freeze to death before I could drown. I did the best sightings I could do to ensure I was in the exact middle, placed my hand in the loop I had made in the boulder, and pushed it off the raft. I, of course, went with it. And the water was COLD. If possible, it was even colder than before. Fortunately, this time I was more prepared and didn't gasp. I just clenched up as the boulder and I dropped like a stone (get it?) to the bottom of the pond.

We hit the bottom what felt like ten minutes later relatively softly. I was already frozen, drowning, almost unable to move, and starting to panic. Then I saw it. Fortunately, the water was so clear it was no darker down here than it was on shore. Right next to me—thank goodness the boulder hadn't landed on it— was a rock on the bottom of the pond. It looked for all the world like a book that had been singed and had the numbers one through nine raised on its cover. Seriously? I'm about to die and the bitch gives me another puzzle?

If possible, I liked that bitch even less.

Since I was freezing, drowning, and feeling ironic, I pushed numbers four, five, and one, in order, and slowly began to lose consciousness. At least that was the plan. What actually happened was the boulder and I fell through a doorway that hadn't been there a second ago and we landed hard on a stone floor some ten feet below.

I lay there freezing and dying and coughing and crying (yes, I'm a girl and I cry, AGAIN that doesn't make me weak, it just makes me a young girl who cries, get over it). After an indeterminate time spent shivering, the warmth started to seep into my bones, if not my hair. The room felt like it was well over a hundred degrees but since I was most likely hypothermic at this point, I figured it was probably cooler.

I slowly took stock of my surroundings, trying not to miss anything. I was in a land of endless riddles and missing even the slightest clue would probably kill me.

Let's see. I was in a round room with four torches lighting it. The room was maybe twenty feet in diameter and ten feet high. The ceiling was solid above me. Even the opening I had fallen through was gone. At that point it also occurred to me that no water had fallen through with me. I don't know why that bothered me so much, but it did. This land was seriously weird in a dangerous, you-might-die-any-second sort of way.

Anyway, the torches were evenly spaced. There was what appeared to be a natural shelf with another stone book on it on the wall to my right. That was a little on the nose for me but what are you going to do? I didn't design the place.

I walked over and looked at the book. There were three raised numbers again, but this time the numbers were "one,'" "three," and "five." The book's title was "Choose Right or Die." Well, that was ominous and not the least bit helpful. None of those numbers were "right." After all, none of them were my lucky number. So, choose Right or Die, which number was right? Hmm. . .. Oh, crap. Use your head, girl. I pushed in the number five because that was the number on the right. The book opened.

Page one read: "Choose wisely this time or meet a villain most foul." Villain most foul? What, was I in some sort of bad novel or something? Since I did not want to meet anyone that mean, I chose the number three. After all, the mean of those three numbers was three.

The page turned. Okay. That one seemed a little weak for someone who is supposed to be a puzzle-maker but what can you do? At least I survived.

"Only one number left, so choose right again." Well, that one was easy. I chose five again. Behind me I heard a horrible shriek. Assuming I'd chosen wrong, I spun quickly and drew one of my knives to face a villain most foul, only to see an opening that hadn't been there before.

I walked to the opening and studied it carefully for more traps. Nothing in this cave was going to be easy. On the left side of the opening was a carving of a beautiful Mallard. It was a great bird with beautiful plumage, but that probably wasn't the answer. I studied it for a few more minutes but didn't see anything other than the obvious, so I "ducked" as low as I could get and went through the opening. As I went through, the top half of the door slammed tight, so I figured I'd passed this test.

Well, this isn't fun, I thought, as I walked down the hall to a large, open room. It looked identical to the room I had fallen into, except no hole in the ceiling. It was round, and four torches lit it. It was the same maybe twenty feet in diameter and ten feet high, which made me smile as I wondered if she got a deal on rooms like this.

Okay, back to, you know, paying attention, and trying not fall into some stupid trap and die. The only thing inside the room was a chess set. Each piece was about half again my height. There weren't many left on the board. On the wall were the words, "Black to move." Oh, my, I hadn't played much chess in my life. This was going to take a few minutes to figure out.

Probably two hours later, I was completely stumped. Black had to move next. I assumed I had to win. But no matter what move I made, mate in three moves was going to be the best possible outcome. Jim Valvano always said never give up. Those were words to live by. On the other hand, Sun Tzu said the opportunity to defeat an enemy would be provided by the enemy. I wasn't here to win this game. I was here to talk to Ariadne.

I went to the board and tipped over the black king. Under it was a small ball of string that looked to be made of an infinite amount of tiny threads woven into a ridiculously complex knot.

"Well done, child, well done," sang a voice that was beautiful, sad, joyous, and mysterious all rolled into one. I could listen to that voice forever. "Almost none make it to me. Take this string with you. Tie it around your finger and it will lead you through Mobious' lands without fail. You may go now, with my warmth and blessing. I will warn you, though. This ring can never leave this land. And if you put it on your finger it will never unravel. You may well be in this land forever."

Well, that sucked . . . a lot. But I had a mission. When problems got this big the only thing to do was solve the first one and then move on to the next. If I tried to solve them all at once I would be stuck forever.

"I thank you." I looked down and wrapped the string on my finger. "Someday I will return this to you." I looked up, but no one was there.

That seemed a tad rude, but she was a goddess, what can you do? I doubt she gave any craps at all about anyone's attitude toward her. Gods and honey badgers. With that cheery thought, I examined the string, which was now a perfectly fitting ring on my finger and made my way back to the room where this all started. There was a hole in the top of the cave and I could see water above it that was so clear it was almost transparent. Crap, I forgot about this part. I couldn't possibly swim up through that freezing water. I hoped when Ariadne gave me her "warmth and blessing" that she had meant it literally. I leapt up through the hole and into the bottom of the pond.

She had. The water was as warm as a soothing bath. There was firm sand below me where the hole I leaped through had been a moment ago. The book was gone but the raft was still there, so I had my bearings. Swim twenty feet or so straight up, over to the shore, get my gear, and head out. Easy-peasy.

Ha! It actually was. The water felt so nice I swam back, instead of using the raft. Then, I retrieved my stuff, grabbed some food from my bag, rebuilt my fire and settled in for a very brief nap. Apparently, I had been down there longer than I thought.

10
THE HAMLET OF HAMLET

After not enough sleep I woke up surprisingly refreshed, cut Stagger Lee loose, and left without a goodbye . . . just kidding.

I woke up in the grasslands feeling refreshed and as if I was finally moving forward. Evidently, Ariadne's ring cancelled out

Mobius' loop. So now, just keep walking forward. Eventually, I would get there. At least I had found a road, so I knew I was going somewhere "road worthy."

A day later the grassland began to give way to large farms. They looked well-maintained but the people were none too friendly. I waved and gave greetings to everyone I passed but they kept working and carefully did not look my way. A couple of dogs came out close to the road and barked and growled at me. I was not too worried about that, though. Dogs seemed instinctively to fear me ever since the accident. I knew from experience that they were much more likely to run away with their tail between their legs if I approached than attack or beg for food or belly rubs. It was a little sad but what can you do? I am not going to cry about dogs. I'm really not.

Around midday (I had nine to twelve days left depending on Mobius and what he did to time other than my own, if you're keeping count), I topped a small hill and saw a hamlet a few hundred yards in the distance. There weren't a lot of buildings, it being a hamlet and all. I saw what appeared from the distance to be a stable, an inn, a general store, a jail, and a couple other buildings with less obvious designations. Everything looked to be relatively neat and tidy. People moved about doing whatever people in hamlets do at midday.

By people, I mean just that. There did not appear to be any

intelligent boars or that sort of thing. Just people, and even from a distance I could see they were not very tall. I would probably be average height or better even for a man in this place. That would be odd, and somewhat satisfying.

Having gleaned all I could from a distance, and hungry for information, and hungry for anything that didn't taste like my energy bars (or pig), I made my way into town in search of sustenance for the body and mind.

While the town was not a bustling metropolis by any standard, a couple of things immediately stood out as I entered it. First, all the buildings (except for the jail) were made of wood and they seemed very sturdy and well-built. And b, I was not attracting much attention. This was good as I didn't have any clothes that I thought would help me fit in. As I looked around more carefully, I began to see why. Most of the people wore standard peasant attire, the men wore sturdy pants and woolen shirts and the women wore simple dresses. However, some men wore leather that wasn't too far removed from my wardrobe and the occasional woman did wear pants. Fitting in apparently wasn't going to be as hard as I feared.

"You there!" cried a deep voice to my left. "Stand where you are."

Me and my big thoughts. I should have known nothing was easy in this world, land, realm, wherever the heck I was.

Anyway, I turned slowly and studied the man rapidly approaching me in a somewhat comical rolling gate. He was maybe three inches shorter than me and five to seven times as thick. I guessed there was muscle under all that fat at one time, but those days were long gone. His beady eyes and attempt at a scowl told me the rest of the story. This was a man who had more insecurities than clogged arteries and was constantly looking to show the world he was in charge.

"What is your business in Hamlet?" he asked with the air of a person who thought he was very important.

I hesitated and smiled. Two things I knew I should not do but he had caught me off guard. "Your hamlet's name is Hamlet?"

"Of course it is, girl. Couldn't you read the sign on your way in?" Then he looked at me suspiciously. "Or did you sneak in? Answer me," he nearly yelled.

"Well, good sir," I said, trying to remember my manners and defuse the situation that I had somehow created. "I do not believe there was a sign. I came in on the main road and am certain I would have seen one."

"Those damn kids," he said angrily. That appeared to be his default state. "I'll deal with them later. But you, state your business in Hamlet."

"My business, sir? Well, that is simple. I am merely passing through. I am seeking the Bull King and am looking for food, rest, and directions, in any order. Perhaps you can assist me? You seem to be a man who knows Hamlet and its people and would certainly know where these things could be found." I was hoping to sound impressed by the little weasel.

It worked! One point for manners!

"I do indeed, young miss," he said, puffing out his fat chest to the point where I thought his shirt might fail. "That building two up the road on the right is the only decent inn in town. Food and drink can be had there. Information? Well, the crowd there can be rough, what with the boars coming into town and all. They are in a foul mood and I would advise you not to speak to them. In fact, I would advise you to listen to everyone there but not to speak to many of them." He nodded knowingly.

"Wait," I said, trying my best not to giggle. Hold steady, girl. "Did you just paraphrase *Hamlet* to me in your Hamlet? And this inn. Is it known as Horatio or something?"

"Are you daft, girl?" he asked with a little bit of heat. "I don't know what you are talking about. The inn doesn't have a name. It's just the inn. Now, I've got a town to see to, being the mayor and all, and you seem to be innocent enough, if a bit slow, so off with you." He pushed around me and walked away with an air of importance.

At least, I am sure that was his thought. It is hard to look important while waddling.

I walked slowly to the inn, trying to gather my thoughts and emotions and was suddenly nearly in tears. Yes, tears. Maybe it was the stress of all this. I mean, new world, Faerie is real, ten or so days left to save seven kids from dying, maybe not even ten. Stupid Mobius. And yes. I'm a teenaged girl and I cry. I don't always know why I am crying. It's just something I have to deal with. I figured out a while ago it doesn't make me weak. I know I keep saying that. Daddy always told me to repeat truths to myself until I believed them.

And crying does *not* make a person weak. It does, on the other hand, make others (men!) sometimes think that I'm weak. Screw them, anyway. If they had to deal with half the crap women had to deal with, they'd be whiny puddles of goo. Of course, if they had to deal with everything we did, there would be better medication, more understanding, and bras that actually fit comfortably. Now that would be something!

With that thought cheering me up, I pushed (a) the tears away and (2) through the doors, then stood there for a second taking it all in. The first thing that hit me was the smell. After a few days in the wonderful air of Faerie, the air in here was almost overwhelming. The scent of stew cooking over a large fire smelled wonderful but it was mixed with the smell of stale, spilled beer and wine, unwashed human bodies, pig musk, smoke, and the pheromone stinks of despair, desperation, and excitement that seem to be universal to drinking establishments. I mean, so I've heard. I had spent a lot of time in gastro pubs as Mama and Daddy loved them. I hadn't spent any time in real bars but that is how Daddy always described them.

The inn itself seemed larger on the inside than it looked before I entered. I don't think it was magic or anything, it was just good lighting combined with proper placement of tables and chairs. There were sixteen tables spaced evenly throughout. A very large fireplace made of stone sat in the middle of the back wall. It was easily large enough to roast an entire cow, although I doubt there was much bovine roasting in these lands. You know: king who is a bull? Instead, it held what appeared to be a deer roasting wonderfully and dripping fat into the fire. Off to the side of the fireplace was a stewpot sitting over smoking coals.

All the tables and chairs were made of some sturdy wood that was probably local to the area. They would have sold for a small fortune in Chicago, but here they were just furniture. Well-built furniture. They'd make pretty good weapons, unlikely to break in a fight. The floor was wood as well, with a light coat of sawdust to soak up the inevitable spills and to give better traction. The four tables to my left and two in the center were filled with anywhere between four and six people. Most of them glanced up at me and quickly back down to their stews and ales, dismissing me as just another traveler.

There were people at two of the tables in the middle, closest to the fire but they looked more rugged somehow. It was not as if the people on the left appeared weak, they were definitely people used to hard work, but the people in the middle had the bearing of fighting men. I say men because it appeared that I was going to be the only female in the inn who was not serving food or drink.

It was the tables to the right that concerned me most. Two of them were empty and two of them had been pushed together to allow for the eight boars to sit together. Six of them faced out toward the inn and two were at the sides. None of them had their back to the inn or the door. A couple of them looked at me with open hostility and I saw one lean over and whisper to the boar in the middle, who was by far the biggest of the group and had to bend over quite a bit to hear what they were saying. They evidently didn't count on my super-hearing because I heard him quite clearly telling the big one that I was the one who had attacked them by surprise and freed their prisoner.

I guess that is why they were in here, rather than dining on Stagger Lee Soup.

Oh, well, not my problem. I assumed they wouldn't start

anything in town, or at least not right away and I was here for information. It did change my plans to maybe sleep in a bed for a few hours, assuming of course the bed was mostly insect-free. Most insects did not bite me for some reason, but still, ugh.

I made my way to one of the center tables and put my back to the fireplace. It was a tad too warm, but it did give me a view of the entire room and no one would be able to get behind me without being very obvious about it.

"What can I get for you?" asked a young woman who appeared to take my order. I studied her for a second. Her hair was golden. Not blond like mine, but golden. It was really pretty and fell to her shoulders. She had a sturdy build that spoke of honest work, but she did not carry herself like a fighter of any kind, so I relaxed.

"That stew smells wonderful," I said, because it did. "I would like a large bowl of it, a large slice of what is roasting over the pit, and some water, if it is clean. If not, bring me wine. Also, bread would be nice."

She looked at me for a moment and said in a small voice, "Stew, meat, and wine do not come cheap, my lady. I hesitate to ask, but do you have coins to pay? I am sorry to ask but I can get in a lot of trouble if I bring things to those who cannot pay."

She looked like she was going to shrink into a puddle of fear which made me very angry; not at her, of course, but at anyone who would hurt this child. Honestly, she only looked a couple years younger than me, but I had lived a lot earlier than she had. "That is a fair question, young miss. I must admit I am not familiar with the currency here." I opened my coin purse and let most of the coins I had gathered from the pigs spill out. "Is there enough here?"

The coins spilling out got the reaction that I'd hoped for from the patrons at the inn. I now saw much more interest in me. This would help me get the information I needed much faster. The boars' reaction was more interesting. I expected to see avarice and predator. I mostly saw anger. Odd.

"Dear me, Miss," the waiting girl exclaimed. "Do not flash such a fortune around in here. It will be nothing but trouble. That one coin there," she said, pointing to a small disk of what looked to me to be something like silver, but definitely not silver, "that coin there will pay for your dinner and drinks and a room for at least three days."

Wow, I had a lot more than I thought. I had at least ten of those coins and I didn't think they were the most valuable ones I had. "Tell me, then," I said with a smile, "what coin or coins will get me food and drink and a bed for tonight that is private and clean?"

"Why, three of those little copper ones will do that just fine."

"Excellent, then. Take them"—I handed her four— "and take

one for you and bring me stew, meat, bread, and wine, since you seemed hesitant about the water. The fourth one in your hand now is for you to keep."

"Thank you so much!" she somehow exclaimed quietly.

Now that was a skill I was going to have to learn. She quickly headed off and was back in a matter of minutes with hot stew in a large wooden bowl, warm bread, and a pitcher of wine that didn't smell bad at all, and a slab of meat the size of my head. Perhaps this would finally be a night where I could enjoy a good meal. My energy bars were not running low yet, but it never hurts to stretch things out.

I started shoveling the delicious stew into my mouth. The flavor was wonderful. It was all vegetables, and a little thin, but like nothing I had ever tasted. There were flavors in it I am quite certain did not exist where I am from. The bread melted in my mouth and the wine was sweet but shy of being cloying. It was very similar to one Mama liked a lot, but somehow cleaner, more flavorful. I was more familiar (I think) than most people my age with various alcohols. Daddy used to sip Blanton's at night and drink whatever Three Floyds was making most of the time. He thought it was better to let me have a drink or two with him than to think alcohol was something mysterious and wonderful, so I had at least some familiarity with different types of alcohol.

Anyway, back to the meal. The meat was just short of medium rare and wonderful. I was truly settling in and feeling good for a change when I saw one of the boars at the end of the table grab the serving girl roughly and push her against the wall.

Dang it all, can't a girl have one peaceful moment? I got up and walked purposefully toward the boar holding the girl. I didn't hurry or try to attract any attention until I was only about a foot behind him. I saw the boars at the table look toward their leader, but he just shook his head and they settled in nervously to watch. Well, one-on-one was much better odds than I had hoped for.

I tapped him on the shoulder, and said, "Excuse me," as politely as I could. My voice sounded much sweeter than I thought it would, given my anger. "This young lady was fetching me more wine and you are interfering with my meal. Why don't you just let her get about her business and we can forget what an ass you are making of yourself and we can all get back to a pleasant evening?"

Surprisingly, he let go of the girl and turned to face me. I guess I assumed he had more bullying and dominance-assertion to complete with her before moving to me. But, no. He was a bully who hated being interrupted. He was about a foot taller than me and had ugly tusks that looked razor-sharp. I could see his anger building at being interrupted by someone smaller and more helpless than himself.

I took a half step back and waited. He was going to swing on me, that much was obvious, so I just waited. Strangely, I saw him look over my head, presumably at his leader, and he hesitated. He must have finally gotten a go-ahead because he reared back to give me a looping right hand. Seriously, he reared back. How bad a fighter was this guy to give me a tell like that? Well, that would make things a lot easier.

I waited until he was in full rear back, stepped in, and pushed his right shoulder enough to send him back into the wall. Then put my hand around his thick throat and held him there. "It doesn't feel very good to be helpless, does it?" I asked with some heat. "Maybe you should remember that before picking on little girls." He reached for a dagger with his other hand, but I already had one out and placed it between his legs at an upward angle. "I believe the term is barrow," I said. "Perhaps you're heard it. If your hand lowers another inch, you will live it."

He gave me a very puzzled look, which was not at all what I was going for, so I tried again. "Capon? No? Stag? No? SERIOUSLY? How about: 'Pig formerly known as the guy with testicles?"

Finally, he seemed to understand as he eased his hand away

from his dagger and put it over his head. The other joined it. Males of any breed are easy to tame. Once, of course, they actually understand the threat.

"That will be enough," I heard from the table behind me, the voice deep and confident. It spoke of authority that was not used to being questioned and a calm that stated that those who did question it did not do so more than once.

"Put down the knife, Outlander, and this does not have to get any worse for you. Although I'm not certain at this point how much worse it can get," he said with almost a laugh, "but let's try not to find out until I've at least finished eating."

"Your thug here is lacking in manners," I said without turning around. Hopefully, I was speaking as calmly as he did.

There was no need to turn around, really. I could hear that no one had moved at the table of boars. The rest of the bar had pretty much cleared out except for the fighting men in the middle of the inn. They were just sitting there carefully not drawing attention to themselves while they took it all in.

"Deputy Johansonn will not be a problem," he said from behind me. "By the way, that is Deputy Johansonn you are holding at knife point, at the moment."

Oh, crap. Deputy? This can't be good.

"Now why don't you come here and have a pleasant conversation before this turns into something none of us want.

It's still not too late for this to all work out."

Double crap. I was starting to get the feeling I had badly misjudged the situation. Well, Munchkins sometimes do rush in where the intelligent dare not follow.

I let go of Deputy Johansonn, who gave me a nasty look until he realized that I hadn't sheathed my knife yet. Once that dawned on him, I put the knife back into the leg slit I had drawn it from and went over to the table. I deliberately turned my back on him to show him that I did not consider him a threat, but I did keep an ear on him to make sure he didn't try anything stupid. Then I pulled up a chair across from the boar who had spoken. It put my back to the door but ensured I could keep this entire group in my sightline.

"So," the big boar said. "I assume you are the one they are calling The Bandit Munchkin? The one who attacked my people without provocation and freed a known cheat and murderer they had been tracking for weeks? I cannot say that it is a pleasure to meet you. I will say, though, based on the shape of my people when I found them, I thought you'd be bigger."

Triple crap. This was not going at all the way I pictured it in my head. Of course, how often had that happened since I got here "I'm sorry, Officer . . .?" I hesitated until I got a name.

"Eckridgeson," he said with something of a smile. He was either way overconfident, or I was in a lot of trouble.

"Officer Eckridgeson," I continued. "But it seems to me that you have been told a very different version of what happened than the one I remember. As I recall, I was merely walking through the forest when I saw some of your people here by a campfire. They had a man trussed up in a sack and were preparing to eat him. You hear me? EAT HIM!" I said with more than a little heat.

I mentally shook myself and calmed down. I realized that I was half prepared to come out of my seat, and relaxed. After all, he neither moved, nor seemed to notice my anger all that much.

He shook his head. "You are sadly misinformed, young miss. What I see is a naive outlander who gave way to her uninformed prejudices and attacked officers of the law performing their rightful duties. It seems to me you are in a lot of trouble." His voice had adopted the tone Daddy always used when he was disappointed in something I had done, and I started to feel bad for a moment before I remembered the whole, *They-were-going-to-eat-a-person* thing.

"Nope, not how it happened. I distinctly heard them say that they were going to eat him."

"Little miss," he said with some exasperation. "We are vegetarians. Look at the table. Not a scrap of meat to be seen. We would never tolerate the eating of another living being. We . . .." His voice trailed off and I saw anger building. "Damn it! Did you guys do that whole 'We're going to kill you then cook you then eat you' thing? I've told you before to stop that nonsense before you spread too many bad rumors. It's bad enough being the pigs who enforce the law without stupid rumors flying about!"

He was really mad, and thankfully it wasn't at me. Which was good. I had a feeling I definitely did not want him mad at me, especially the way everyone around him started to cower and look away.

"Okay," I said. "It seems there was a misunderstanding. I am very sorry for that. But really? Would you stand by if you thought someone was going to be eaten by a band of ruffians? It's not as if I knew they were officers of the law or anything. They weren't wearing badges and never identified themselves." I hesitated for a moment as what I had done sank in. "I am truly sorry. I would never have attacked them if I had known and I definitely would never have killed anyone if I hadn't been fighting for my life."

He looked puzzled for a second or two and then smiled. "You really aren't from around here, are you?"

I shook my head.

"You didn't kill anyone. It is really hard to do that here. You carved a few of my boys up good but they were right as rain once they limped off to a healer. Even an arrow to the chest is not fatal if a decent healer is close enough. I still have a problem with you, though. Knowingly or not, you helped a criminal escape, assaulted officers of the law, then did it again here in the bar, in front of witnesses. I cannot just overlook that. It would make people think they can flaunt the law at will and just claim ignorance. Now," he said leaning forward, "just what should I do with you?"

"Well," I replied, "how about banishment? I am on my way out of town anyway."

"And just where are you heading?"

I didn't think I should tell him that I was heading to kill the guy who was most likely his king, so I replied, "I believe I am heading east. But perhaps you can help me there. I am looking to find the Bull King and I believe his cattle, er, castle, is that way?"

"East?" he replied while thinking. "Perhaps that will work out best for everyone. Yes, the castle is that way, but you will have to pass through the Centaur Woods to get there. Either that or detour around it and it would take you weeks longer. Now, I've never heard of anyone actually passing through there alive so, as much as it makes me feel like a secondhand murderer, I suppose I could banish you." He waited a moment to finish his thoughts. "A perfect solution for all. You are banished starting tomorrow after breakfast. You will head out with all alacrity and not return. Agreed?"

"Sorry to be a pest," I pestered, "but can I do some quick shopping in the morning to replenish supplies?"

"Very well. Anything to be out of this situation. You are banished as of midday tomorrow."

"One more thing," I said, and he started looking angry. I really didn't care, though. This one more thing was going to get done.

"That *officer* on your left," I said with a lot of heat. "He pretty much threatened to rape me. Now, I gave him a pretty stern lesson on trying that kind of disgusting nonsense with me, but I seriously doubt that I am the first female he's ever tried that with. So, tell me, *Officer*," I said putting as much emphasis on the word as I could, "what do you do with would-be rapists in these lands?"

He looked furious. And I mean, he looked as if he was going to break the table in half. "Is what she says true, Pepridgeson?"

My would-be rapist started to back out his chair while exclaiming, "No, sir! Never! I'd never do such a thing!"

"Hold him," he ordered the two of his men to the left. He looked at me for a long moment. "Do you so swear? On your life and honor? On the honor of your family that this person had this intention?"

"I do," I said with the force of a vow I actually felt. "He said to be quiet because he did not want to share."

"I only meant share her valuables," he cried out.

The captain or whatever, I really should've asked, looked truly furious now. "So, you admit that you were going to rob someone while performing duties of an officer of the law? You admit you were going to do this while performing these duties under my watch?!"

He stood quickly and backhanded the creep so hard I wasn't certain if he had broken his neck. Not that I cared about his neck getting broken, but I did vow to be a little more polite. Oh, yeah, and not ask if they were all deliberately named after sausage meats. That was some serious power in that slap.

He turned and looked at me, trying hard to suppress his anger. "He will be taken to the jail now. If he is lucky the magistrate will just castrate him. If I have my way the losing of his little head will be followed by the loss of his larger one." He turned back to his men. "Take him away."

After a second to compose himself, he turned back to me. "I still expect you gone by midday tomorrow but go with my apologies, young miss."

"Thank you, sir," I replied and left this part of the inn quickly. I found the girl in back and requested a room for the night and to be woken at first light if I hadn't stirred by then. I hated to lose the time, but I hadn't slept more than an hour or two a day since I got here. I trudged up to my room, blew out the candle, blocked the door with a chair, found the bed surprisingly clean, and fell into a deep slumber.

11
THE INEVITABLE ROBBERY

The next morning found me up before the sun and ready to begin the next phase of my journey. I washed up as well as I could and made my way down the stairs for a quiet breakfast of thick porridge and milk. I had the room entirely to myself except for one of the men who had been sitting in the middle of the room the night before. He was lingering over his breakfast but finished quickly when I came down and made his way out the front door.

Oh, well, my fault for flashing all that coin, but I knew the risks when I did it.

I left the inn after leaving a very large tip for the service. My servers had been great, and the food was even better. Besides, if I was going to be robbed later at least some of the money would go to good. Then I went across the street and purchased more supplies. I supplemented my energy bars with jerky and other snacks. I also bought a truly beautiful woven blanket that was just too much of a bargain to pass up. It probably took up a bit too much space in my bag, but I figured I could secure it under my pack just fine. Plus, my recent swim made me wish that I had thought to bring a blanket along. As I had more money than I thought originally, I even considered purchasing a horse. However, that seemed like it might be insensitive. I should have asked the po-po last night about the centaurs' opinion on horses. I didn't feel as if I could fully trust the person who might be selling me a horse, so I had some walking to do. I took one last look around town but apparently Starbucks hadn't made it to this world . . . yet. So, coffee-free, I headed out toward the Centaur Woods.

I walked slowly for the first half hour and was getting impatient. There were small farms as far as I could see, which was a long way right now, and nary a person was in sight. I felt like I was in Nebraska more than Faerie as flat as the land looked heading east. With that boringly cheerful thought, I kept trudging on. But I couldn't wait forever for these jokers, as I had kids to save.

Well, I had stalled enough! They were probably in position by now, and the boars were nowhere to be found. It looked as if it was getting at least close to ambush time, so I picked up my pace while making sure I was as ready as possible.

A couple hours' later and still no attack. As I made my way, the farms got larger and I saw no people at all, not even travelers for at least an hour, so I tried to be even more careful. I began to stop every so often to make sure my weapons were going to be easy draws and loosened my pack so I could drop it quickly.

By the end of the day I was sore from carrying my pack too loose and frustrated by all the waiting. It was starting to get dark, so I moved a couple hundred yards deep into a wheat field while making as few tracks as I could and settled in for a quick rest. I dug no fire, didn't snore (that I know of) and was small enough that lying down I did not think anyone could see me from the road. The night was warm and pleasant (of course) and the ground was soft, so I managed to catch a few hours' sleep in between waking up at every little noise. The bandits were starting to tick me off. Let's get this over with already!

It was still dark when I woke up after too little sleep, ate, took care of the things everyone has to do, that boys find funny for some reason, girls just find gross and necessary, and I was back on the road.

From what I had gleaned in town, I would be at the Centaur Forest well before nightfall so any time soon they would have to attack. At least I hoped so. If I could get through these bandits, the odds were pretty good that I wouldn't see any others, so at least I could walk in peace for a few hours before facing the centaurs. The centaurs were not supposed to be friendly toward people so I assumed walking into the forest tense and stung out from perpetually waiting to be attacked would be seen as either sneaking, or abject stupidity. I wanted to go in as openly and as friendly-looking as possible.

Two hours later, I stopped for a quick snack and was very frustrated with these bandits. I was beginning to think they had a serious lack of commitment to this. I was going to be at the woods soon, or at least that was what I had heard in town. They wouldn't want to attack too close to the centaurs, so they were running out of time. After all, they had to assume that the closer I got to the woods the more alert I would be. Centaurs rarely, if ever, interacted with people outside of the woods. I mean, other than to stick arrows into them. But they were known to chase people off who got too close to the woods. And to beings with hooves designed for running, I had to assume too close for them was farther out than most people assumed.

My guess was as soon as I was in eyeshot of the woods, I would be in what they assumed was, at best, neutral territory. I had watched enough sci-fi to know that the Neutral Zone was not a place of safety and security for either side.

It was an hour or so later when I finally found it. No, not the Centaur Woods, that would be too much to ask for. What I found was a valley. It wasn't much of a valley, but it was the first change to the landscape since I had left town. I was going to have to walk down maybe twenty feet and then back up. Back up was where they would be waiting. If, of course, these people had any work ethic at all. I mean, seriously, they could have at least taken some cover in all this wheat and tried to surprise me hours ago. That would have saved us all a lot of time and effort. But no. These jerks just had to draw it out.

Anyway, I walked down to the bottom of the hill and made a great show of stretching and lounging and basically just wasting time. I wanted a couple of things here. A, I wanted to annoy them as much as they had annoyed me by making me wait, and two, it gave me a second to palm a dagger in my left hand. After killing two minutes or so I walked up the hill to spring the ambush.

I reached the top and perhaps ten paces more when they "sprang." Okay, not really. These guys really did not seem all that professional. Two of them rolled out of the ditch to my right and one to the left. Interesting. That left two more if everyone from the table at the inn was in their gang. I scanned the area as best I could as quickly as I could and found one rising with a bow in his hand perhaps twenty-five yards to the left and one equidistant to the right. I'm sure they thought that was overkill. I was about to show them how underkill it actually was.

"Hold it right there, Traveler!" said the one who had rolled out from the left side. "Place all your weapons and valuables at your feet and you can be on your way. If you are quick enough, perhaps we will even leave you your clothes," he said with an evil leer that gave me no doubt on the odds of that happening.

Some men in any world seemed to think a woman's main purpose was their pleasure. Well, now I was really ticked off. But I didn't want to show it just yet.

"That is an interesting proposition," I said, trying to look like I was thinking it over. "But what assurances do I have that you will keep your word? You are bandits, after all. Bandits are notorious for not keeping their word."

"What?" he asked, obviously puzzled at my lack of fear.

"What do you mean 'what'?" I replied. "Oh," I said, as if understanding had just come to me. "Notorious. It means 'of note.' Like famous or well known. Bandits are not *well known* for keeping their word."

That seemed to upset him, I thought while forcing down a smile. I was more worried about the archers than the men in front of me but, honestly, they did not look as if they were all that skilled. They already had their bows drawn, which meant the longer this conversation went the more tired they would become. They also had horrible form. That might not matter terribly at this distance, but I definitely was not worried about a precision shot to the eye or anything like that, and my jacket should be able to stop anything short of a direct shot.

I can tell you from a lot of experience that a precision shot takes a lot more skill and practice than these people had. Of course, I reminded myself, it would not take a lot of luck or skill at this distance to at least hit me, and then you never know what would happen.

"Do not waste my time or try my patience, girl," he said, as if he were important. "This can go very badly for you if you test me. Now, place all your belongings on the ground. At once!"

"Or?"

"Or what, girl? If you do not obey me immediately, I'll have my men shoot you and then we will take everything off your dead body."

"Okay," I replied reasonably.

"Good, then," he said with a note of satisfaction.

I just stood there waiting for a few moments, giving him a look that Daddy always said only a teenage girl can give. It was a combination of "You are an idiot" and "I cannot believe how much of an idiot you are" with a tad of "What an idiot" thrown in.

"What are you waiting for, girl!" he screamed, and spittle went everywhere. Gross.

"I'm confused. I am not waiting for anything," I replied, trying to sound confused. "'What am I waiting for' what?"

He looked really confused now so I thought I would show some pity on him. "You said your guys were going to shoot me and rob my dead body. Right? Well, that seems preferable to me to what I think you have in mind if I am not dead, so go ahead. Shoot me."

Now he looked really upset. I'm not sure why because he gave me the options and I took one. Daddy always said I that could upset anyone, though, so point for him, I guess.

"Kill her!" he yelled, which is what I had been waiting for. It's much easier to time things when you know they are coming. I took a quick jump forward and another back as the arrows buzzed by, not even close enough for me to feel them. I then took the knife that I'd palmed and threw it into the chest of the man who'd been speaking. It plunked solidly where his heart would be if he had one. I mean metaphorically, of course. He probably had a heart, he just acted like he didn't. Anyway, heart or not, he was most likely out of the battle.

I assumed the "archers" would be nocking more arrows, so I rushed the men to my right. This way the archers would either have to drop their bows and rush me or take a chance on hitting their friends. I hoped they would rush me because I figured there was at least a small chance they could hit a moving target and I liked my odds better with them in close.

Neither of the men I charged had been expecting it for some

reason, so the first one went down quickly when I punched him in the throat and I used the momentum that I had gained to ram into the other and knock him back a few feet.

Okay, "ram" might have been optimistic given my weight, but these guys were at best an inch or two taller than me so at least it knocked him back. He regained his footing and sprang forward with a clumsy slash. Wasn't anyone in Faerie well-trained? I didn't bother to parry with the knife I now had in my right hand. Instead, I spun enough for the slash to miss my stomach and sliced his hand before he could withdraw.

Apparently, I had some adrenaline built up, or Faerie guys were really slender, because his hand almost came off which caused a somewhat comical situation. Blood sprayed the archer who had dropped his bow and was rushing up behind him. He tripped and went over backward as he tried to keep it out of his eyes. That took him out of the action for a moment, so I spun to avoid any oncoming arrows and looked for the other archer.

He was just standing there with his hands in the air, so it looked like he was the smart one. "Go!" I yelled. "Before I have to hurt you." I didn't even bother to see if he would obey. He looked like a puppy that had been caught piddling on the floor, so I knew that he was out of this.

I quickly turned back to the one who had tripped. He was getting to his feet and reaching down for his sword, so I stepped over and kneed him in the chest. As he fell backward, I kicked him between the legs, hopefully hard enough to end his raping days. I felt at least one solid pop, so I knew he was out of this.

Let's see . . . there was one running away. There was one most likely dead. Or at least mostly dead. One was trying desperately to bind his hand and one who looked as if he might never let go of his pride and joys. The one I punched in the throat was gasping and wheezing, but he looked like he'd probably recover. All in all, not a bad few moments' work. I figured they would all heal eventually because it seems as if nothing was too permanent in this land, but I did not really care. I know I am supposed to feel guilty about hurting people but when you bring rape into the picture, you are no longer a person to me. You are a rabid animal that just needs to be put down.

"You there," I said to the man who almost had his hand bound up. "Lefty. Empty Soprano over there's money bag and put it with yours on the ground." As I said that I walked over to Heartless and cut his loose. "After that, I'd suggest you and Wheezy find the smart one and head back to town."

Heartless was beginning to groan, so I took my knife from his chest and cleaned it on his shirt. Looked like he'd live, as well.

"Lefty," I called, and he jumped like I'd beaten him. Which I guess I had. "When you're done over there, grab Heartless here as he still seems to be breathing. One last thing," I said to all of them in my sternest voice. "It seems really hard to kill you guys even with steel, but I swear by all that's holy if I ever see any of you again I will either figure out a way to do it, or make you wish I had."

With that I gathered up the coin purses, threw them into my go-bag, broke both bows that were lying on the ground, and headed off in the direction of the woods without a look back. These guys had all the fight taken out of them so I wasn't too worried about anything except a long-distance attack, and with their bows broken they wouldn't be causing anyone trouble for a little while. Cowards.

12
THE CENTAUR WOODS

Well, the attempted robbery at least broke the monotony. But it did make me wonder if the land of Faerie was made up of people (and sentient animals) that were a lot smaller and less dangerous than I had originally thought. Of course, I quashed that line of thinking because it would definitely jinx me. I mean, sure, jinxes are not real, but does that mean I start counting a Purdue basketball victory when they are up by ten with five minutes to go? Does that mean Daddy never drinks a root beer during the game? After all, root beer is a victory drink, and shouldn't be drunk until you've won. Does that mean washing your car makes it rain or buying a new snowblower stops the snow? Of course not. But then again, why risk it?

With those and other random thoughts running through my brain the last little distance to the forest went quickly. There was a very clear demarcation between the forest and the grassland. Up ahead, maybe one hundred yards, the road just stopped, and a mighty forest stood proudly. It stretched to the north and south as far as I could see. What was interesting was that even the edge of the forest, presumably where the most light would seep in, was old growth. Massive trees soared a hundred feet or more into the sky and smaller trees were hard to find.

Okay, this answered one question I had. What would a bunch of horse-bodied creatures be doing running around a forest when there was so much grassland about? The trees were large enough, and their canopy interlocking enough that smaller trees and bushes would have a hard time growing. There was a nice layer of moss and a few leaves on the ground, but it appeared walking, or even running—which is typically suicide in a forest—would not be a major issue. The only issues I could see were a), no obvious road, and two), no readily apparent way to navigate a relatively straight line. My sense of direction is fine, but I did not want to exit the forest miles to the north or south when everybody just kept telling me "head due east."

Well, Munchkin, when there is no obvious entry, forward

usually seems to work as well as any other direction, I thought. I often call myself Munchkin when I talk to me. I'm not sure why. It's not as if there was anyone else that I could be thinking to. It just seemed natural.

Okay, delving deep into the internal Munchkin wasn't getting me anywhere so maybe stepping into the forest would. As there was no obvious path, I oriented myself as best I could and stepped into the forest at the first convenient spot. The first thing that hit me was the temperature change. I wasn't as if it was cold, just very noticeably cooler than a few steps ago.

The second thing was, like everything else in Faerie, it was beautiful.

I could not see far in any direction. You know, I couldn't see the forest for the trees, but I could see at least far enough to give me comfort that nothing could rush me without giving me some warning, unless, of course, something was hiding behind a tree. I wasn't worried about that unless there were intelligent zombies in the area because I can still hear heartbeats. No, I have never heard of intelligent zombies, but that does not mean they don't exist. Don't be a bigot.

Speaking of hearing, I did hear the chirping of birds and the rustling and chittering of small animals, so the forest was obviously as healthy as it looked. In fact, it seemed very healthy. Much like the grasslands and farms I had just walked through, the air was amazingly clean, and the scenery was just more than in my world. The trees were bigger, and somehow even happier.

If it wasn't for the whole "Kill the Bull King in an unrealistic time frame thing" and occasional robbers and stuff, I could totally take a long vacay here. I hadn't really been out of the facility for a couple of years and I could almost feel the indoor stink leaving my body. But, of course, all this enjoyment of life was not getting me closer to my goal, so I made my way forward and more or less easterly through the woods. I wondered off and on how long I would be in the woods as no one I talked to seemed to have any other than the vaguest idea how big the woods is. From what I gathered it was somewhere between a week's and two months' walk, so really, no clue. Either way, getting through the woods was going to take way too long so I was moving as quickly as I could manage.

About midday when I stopped for a snack and really just to sit for a minute, I heard them. I was sitting at the base of a large tree and checking my equipment when I heard large animals moving in an almost circular pattern. I figured I had either found the centaurs, or some R-O-U-Ses had found me. Since there was not an immediate attack, I was also assuming intelligence and planning were afoot. Well, I needed to meet these guys (guys in the general sense, I was hoping there would be some females with them so there would be someone intelligent to talk to) so I stood up and called out.

Or rather, that was the plan. What actually happened was I started to stand, and a very thick wooden shaft plunked into the tree about six inches above my head. This was followed by two more coming from opposite directions. Okay, then, this was nothing like the bandits I fought before. Those arrows were powerful and fired by beings who knew how to shoot with precision. I could just have easily been a Munchkin kabob.

So, I sat back down, placed my bow carefully on the ground, put my hands on my legs where I would look as harmless as possible, but still be within fast reach of at least two blades, and waited patiently.

A few seconds later, three centaurs came walking slowly out of the trees in front of me. That left at least one that I assumed had to be behind me.

It also meant that planning was a-hoof, rather than afoot. Anyway, I was supportive of the caution even if it did mean that I was in serious trouble if this went sideways. And since nearly every single encounter I had had since entering this land had gone sideways, I could only assume the worst. Since their bows were tucked away, and they now carried spears nearly as long as me with what looked like steel heads—very sharp, very pointy heads—I was assuming "sideways" had arrived.

"Remain seated, little human," came a surprisingly not-deep voice from the centaur in the middle.

I did so and studied him as he came to a stop in front of me. Well, so much for everything in Faerie being smaller and weaker than expected. This dude was huge! The top of my head might be as tall as his deep, chestnut-colored horse back. The male part of him would have fit easily on a guy over six feet tall and he was not skinny. His chest and arms rippled with muscle and there was no body fat on either of his halves. He was hairy except for his face, which looked clean-shaven. His eyes were a dark brown and his hair fell down his back like a mane. He reminded me of that old dude, Duncan MacCleod, that Mama always seemed to like A LOT when she watched old reruns.

The two centaurs flanking him looked enough like him that they could be brothers. Um, siblings? Whatever related horses were called. One was slightly smaller and one larger. However, it was obvious the one in the middle was the oldest and in charge of this situation.

"State your business in our woods, Human."

He said human like it was not a good thing. This was not the pleasant greeting I hoped for.

"Hello, Mr. . . .?" I said with a polite question in my voice. "My name is Anne with an 'e,' but most people call me Munchkin."

I waited with what I hoped was an innocent smile on my face. The smile worked well with human males, but I had no idea how it would go over with centaurs. I hoped it would go over well, but not overly so. I mean, I don't want to be crude or anything, but it was pretty obvious this guy was literally hung like a horse.

"You may call me Gerald," he replied and actually did seem a shade less aggressive. I guess he was satisfied that his was bigger than mine, which really was not much of a competition. "Now, please answer my question, Ms. Munchkin, what exactly are you doing poaching in our woods?"

"Well, Mr. Gerald," I began.

"Excuse me?" he interrupted.

"'Excuse you' what?" was my reply as I had no idea what he had done.

"My name is just Gerald, not Mr. Gerald."

"Oh. Okay then, Just Gerald. I was not poaching or stealing or anything else. I am merely passing through to the east. I will be out of your woods as quickly as I can. Speaking of which, any idea how long that will take me or where I can find the best route?"

"I believe it will perhaps take the rest of your life to leave this woods, Ms. Munchkin," he said ominously. "We do not allow men to trespass on our lands."

"Well, Just Gerald. There does not seem to be an issue," I said, keeping my most innocent smile on my face. "I am not a man."

He looked confused and then a little angry. "I am not certain yet if you are mocking me, or if you are the innocent simpleton you seem. Perhaps I should just be done with you and move on," he said, pointing a long spear at me.

I stood up quickly but did not draw a weapon yet. I didn't like my odds at all against one of these guys, let alone three of them and the one I was relatively certain (I heard rustling as he moved into position for a better shot) was behind me to the left. I was giving up hope of talking my way out of this, or even walking out of this, when the centaur to his left spoke.

"A moment, Gerald," he said in a calm voice that was deeper than his leader's. Just Gerald did not look happy at the intrusion but did hesitate, which I took as a huge win at this point.

"Do not move, Human," he said and turned back to the one on the left who I officially dubbed "Lefty." Just Gerald and Lefty trotted off a dozen feet or so and began talking quietly. I settled in to listen because evidently their idea of quietly was not all that quiet.

Lefty began, "I am not comfortable with this, Gerald. I do not question your leadership, but I would appreciate a moment to talk to you as your younger brother, and as a loyal follower of my herd leader in this." Just Gerald nodded and he continued. "I feel that there is more to this youngling than meets the eyes. She is damn calm and did not seem surprised or scared at all when we approached, or even when we shot arrows by her head. I believe we should take her to the Seer and let her decide her fate."

I could tell Just Gerald did not like either the interruption or the advice, but he hesitated for several seconds and my estimation of him as a leader went way up as he responded, "I disagree, my younger brother, but I do see why you would have such notions concerning her." He smiled in a self-depreciating manner. "Our mother always said that you thought more with your head while I perhaps leaned toward thinking with another part of my anatomy. It shall be as you say."

Wow, a good leader always listens to his people's advice but up until now I had classified Just Gerald as a "little head thinker." Way to go, Munchkin, your prejudices are definitely going to cost you some day.

Just Gerald came trotting back and I waited with a questioning look on my face. "You will come with us, little human. Hold out your hands," he said, producing a rope which I assumed was to tie my hands.

I didn't like that very much, but it beat trying to fight my way out of this. I bent down, secured my bow and other possessions, put my go-bag on my back, and held out my hands. Just Gerald did a thorough job of securing my hands and turned to lead me toward his Seer.

Oh, well, at least the Seer seemed to be east of here.

13
SEEING THE SEER

The main Colt City(?) Bronco Burg(?) Horse Hamlet(?) wasn't too far away. It's hard to tell distances when jogging through the woods but I'd say no more than five miles or so. I didn't want Just Gerald to know that I wasn't very tired or winded at the end of our trot, so I leaned over and pretended to need a minute. I couldn't pretend to sweat but what are you going to do?

Just Gerald must have bought it because he stopped to give me a breather a hundred feet or so short of town and I used the time to study my surroundings. It wasn't very impressive. One large, square, wooden building in the center of town with some kind of very large animal skin, or many very similar skins woven together for walls. Another building perhaps half that size, only it was round and looked to be the centaur equivalent of a bar/restaurant. Loosely surrounding those two buildings were perhaps forty smaller tents, similar to the Native American teepees I saw in museums back home, only, you know, horse-sized.

As I "recovered" two stallions trotted out to us, spears in hand. "Hail and well-met, Gerald," said the larger of the two—the one on the left if you're keeping score. He was truly the larger one. I'm thinking he had a freaking Clydesdale or something in his past. I felt almost like a Hobbit looking at him. "You seem to have brought us a Fae?"

Gerald shook his head. "Well met to you, Clyde. I think it might be a human. There is something unusual about it and we felt perhaps the Seer would like to examine it."

"Excuse me," I said and both of them turned to look at me with surprise and annoyance on their faces. "I am not an it. I am a her, or a she. And yes, I am human. All you had to do was ask and we could have saved a lot of time and I could have been on my way. And is your name really Clyde?" I asked, suppressing both a smile and giggle which I thought showed great maturity and growth on my part.

Clyde the Clydesdale gave a deep, if short laugh, before responding. "I see your point, Gerald. It does not show proper fear or even understanding of its predicament. We will take it, excuse me, *her*," he said, turning to me and smiling, "to the Seer."

With that they trotted toward a larger tent close to the middle of Centaur Center, as I dubbed it, and politely asked me to wait. Just kidding. Clyde told me either sit and be quiet until he came back or the two centaurs guarding me would make me wish I had.

Looking at them, I had little doubt that they could, so I decided to wait meekly. In fact, I was so meek I was almost asleep when Clyde the Clydesdale came back out. "The Seer will see you in the main building. Let's go."

It was a short walk to the main building, and we walked to the center, in front of a stage that was raised perhaps five feet in the air. There was no place to sit and I was trying to figure out how a centaur could possibly get up on the stage when she slowly walked in from the other side. Well, that answered that pressing question. There was a ramp.

She examined me and I returned the favor. She was old, maybe ancient. I don't know how old that meant for a centaur, but she was definitely in her declining years. However, her steps were sure, and her look was confident. Old she may be, but she was still healthy. Her mane was almost pure silver and her face, on a human, would be of a lady in her eighties or nineties. Her eyes were an incredible light blue and they almost seemed to glow. She wore a leather bra that answered two more questions. One, do centaur women wear bras? And b, were they as well-endowed as they were always drawn? The answer to both was a resounding yes. I was never what even a gracious person would call well-endowed, and I never let that bother me (too much), but this lady was stacked! I guess I just assumed because most of the pictures were drawn by boys, and, you know, *boys*, that there was exaggeration. Apparently not.

She caught me looking and gave me a grandmotherly smile. "Fear not, child. There is time enough for that. But tell me, Gerald, why did you bring her to me?" she said, never taking her eyes off me. "Oh, I see." Gerald started to speak but she waved him off. "What are you, girl? Come closer."

I started to climb up on the stage and Just Gerald grabbed my arm. Wow. He was really strong. And I'm not talking Chris Hemsworth strong (or cute). I'm talking about the love child of

The Mountain and Jessica Fithen strong. I would say strong as a horse but that seems a little on the nose. Anyway, I was suddenly very glad I hadn't pushed him more. I may still be stronger, but it was a much nearer thing than I originally thought.

"Enough, Gerald," came the kindly voice from the stage above. "This child won't seek to harm me, will you, child?" she asked with a kindly smile to match her voice.

There was something about her that made me wonder if I could hurt her. She had such a presence, and internal strength. Magic or not, this was someone to be listened to, and not to be underestimated.

"No, ma'am," I said politely as I shook loose from Just Gerald, climbed the stage, and walked toward her. She was not nearly as big as the men. I wondered if that was typical, but since I hadn't seen other females, there was no way to know but ask. And I couldn't think of a polite way to ask.

Anyway, my head came just to about her stomach and she placed her hands on my cheeks the way Mama used to. It brought up a flood of emotions that I did not want to deal with right then. Interestingly enough (at least to me), I think she was the one bringing up my emotions. I didn't care. It was obvious she was not hurting me. Her touch was soothing, and felt like comfort, safety, and home.

But then she suddenly pulled back as if shocked. "What manner of predator are you?" she nearly hissed.

Just Gerald and his friend both reared back to throw spears and I was starting to think "*Crap,*" when the Seer stopped us all from moving. Not literally. Or maybe literally. I don't know. It was weird. Just Gerald and his partner just lowered their spears and their heads.

I didn't lower my head, but it was more out of stubbornness than anything else. I really wanted to bow to her. I'm not sure if it was magic, just supreme confidence, or an understanding that she would be obeyed, along with the realization that she should be obeyed, but she somehow stopped us all without really doing anything but wanting us to stop.

"Again," she said, slipping back into her kindly voice, "what are you, child?"

"I don't know what you mean," I replied, honestly confused. "I'm just a girl, no doubt."

She looked puzzled for a second, so I guess she wasn't a music fan. I continued, "I mean, really. I take pills that keep me at my peak, or maybe a lot more, but that's about it." She did not look convinced and that made me sad and really wanting to convince her. "Seriously, that's it. Maybe that is what you are sensing? Feeling? Smelling?"

"Show me one of your pills," she said in a voice that was still somehow crazy kind and yet totally in control.

I took off my go-bag and began to reach in it when Just Gerald raised his spear, and said, "Stop. Do not reach into that bag in her presence."

I hesitated but she countered, "Enough, Gerald. This child is no danger to me," and I realized that I wasn't. I'm still not sure if that was magic, or just her natural presence.

"Now, child, show me one of your pills, if you please. Gerald, calm yourself or wait outside."

I handed her one of my pills. She smelled it, crushed it, and smelled it again. Then she passed her hand on top of the powder and it glowed a soft orange. She smiled and nodded to herself, then turned to me. "You have been deceived, youngling, these pills do little more than keep your sugar level very high. I can see how that would be valuable for one with your metabolism, but they are not magical by any means."

"Wait, what? One with my metabolism? What does that mean?" I was in tears again. Yeah, I know. Get over it. You're going to hear a lot about tears if the person telling the story is a teenage girl. "What do you mean? What do you know? Please!"

"I do not know the completeness of it," she said kindly. "You are a mixture, a hybrid, something special and new. I can tell you this. You are definitely a predator. That is why some have the reaction to you that they do. They can sense it. I am sure your tale is one for the ages, but I also do not think you know it yet. So, instead of the past, tell me of the now. You are not from here and yet here you are. Why have you come to our woods?"

I hesitated but could somehow tell there would be no use in equivocating. She would see right through it. "I am here for the Bull King. He is killing children and I am going to stop him."

She studied me long enough to make me uncomfortable before replying, "Okay, then." She turned to Gerald. "Feed this child. Get her a place to rest. She will continue her mission in the morning."

Just Gerald did not look happy. Well, neither was I, but he started speaking before I could protest the delay. "She entered our domain. The law is clear. No human or Fae may see our stronghold without permission, and only before it is to be moved."

The Seer looked at Just Gerald and was not happy. "And are you then questioning my decision?" It sounded like a question but really was not. Her look and tone clearly said, "Back off," but Just Gerald was just not budging. Perhaps I'd been a tad too snarky with him.

"No," replied Just Gerald with almost a sound of fear. Not quite, but he knew he was asking for trouble that he might not want. "I am not questioning you. I am merely stating ancient law and wisdom."

"I am familiar with them both, having been consulted on them so many times," she replied with a calm that I wasn't entirely sure she was feeling. She was not used to being questioned so abruptly, or at all. "This child is not human, or at least only partly, and is at best part Fae. She is also something else, something she will have to find out for herself. So, the law concerning those species does not apply to her."

Just Gerald looked happy to have an out. "I would ask then, what is she? If she can tell us that she is neither Fae nor human I will, of course, bow to your wisdom."

She started to reply again but I decided to step in. Probably not my smartest move, but then again, on the list of dumb things I have done this week, including diving into a freezing pond on a hunch, I figured this didn't even crack the top five.

"I thought I was human, Just Gerald." I saw a smirk from the Seer at the name I had given him. "I cannot tell you what I am." Tears began to fall freely, and I didn't care. "I had a Mama and a Daddy. They were both human. I mean, I think, or thought they were.

"They *were* human, darn it! I am not saying the Seer is wrong, but as far as I know, or knew, I am human. But if it isn't the pills, then I don't know. I just don't know."

The Seer came forward, bent down, and wrapped her arms around me. I fell into her arms and sobbed.

"Then I suggest we convene a full council," Just Gerald said.

I knew the Seer was really ticked off by the way her muscles contracted, but now that had I stepped in and opened my big, stupid mouth, she was willing to see where this went. Oh, so that was wisdom, knowing when to shut the heck up. I should probably remember that.

"I believe we can convene one in a week's time. She can stay here, under guard, until then," concluded Just Gerald.

"What?" I sort of shouted. "I don't have a week's time to waste. There are lives at stake here. Also, I need to get home at some point. It's not as if this place hasn't been a basket full of puppies fun, but I have responsibilities."

"Then you should not have trespassed," Just Gerald said, raising up to his full height and crossing his arms over his large chest.

"Enough," the Seer said. "Gerald, you claim this child to be human, correct?" He nodded. "Child, I say you are something else and not bound by the portion of the law Gerald is trying so hard to preserve."

She looked at me and I saw Just Gerald wince out of the corner of my eye. He seriously needed an out here.

I nodded.

"Then I suggest a trial by combat," she stated.

14
TRIAL BY COMBAT

Just Gerald suddenly looked immensely pleased and I revised
my stupidity of interrupting back into the top five, maybe up to

number one.

"Child, as the challenged, you get to pick the event. Gerald, as challenger you pick the time and location."

Interesting. I pick the event. So, it did not have to be direct combat. I already knew what I wanted but I needed Just Gerald to agree. Agitating him might work. It was my go-to in any case.

"Okay, I pick rope-climbing."

Just Gerald looked just ticked off but that was sort of the idea.

"No? Ice Skating? No? Rollerblades? No? Handstands? No, again? Geesh, Just Gerald, you are hard to please."

"Pick something that proves you are not human, Human. Or one you believe you can actually win," he said, and he was really mad.

"Fine, then," I said with mock resignation. "I pick target archery. Not shooting at each other," I added hastily. "Surely no human can beat a centaur at archery, especially at a distance. Will that suffice, my overly finicky opponent?"

"Ha!" he nearly barked. "Archery, indeed. Once you have lost at that I will move that you be summarily beheaded. I choose tomorrow morning, shortly after first light. Five targets to range from twenty to two hundred meters. Winner of each shot to be decided by closest-to-the-spider." He crossed his arms in front of himself again. "Will that suffice, little human? Can you even shoot an arrow two hundred meters? I wouldn't want to take advantage of you."

I replied while trying to hide a smile. "I'll do my best, Just Gerald. But being a small and helpless girl and all, it won't be easy." I saw the Seer try to hide a smile at that, and continued, "Two things: One, can we do this now, and b, I would like to see the range before we start the actual competition. Oh, yeah, and when did the centaurs move to the metric system? Let's get on with this. I need to win and win quickly so I can avoid being beheaded by a Sumerian."

Just Gerald looked confused, but the older centaur laughed and ended the discussion. "Gerald, have someone show the child the range. Also, have them set up a tent by mine and bring her food and water so she may rest before tomorrow's event." She turned to me. "Hurry or not, you need your rest. This will be a fair competition. I will be present to judge."

With that she turned, interestingly enough, not even waiting to see if we'd follow all her commands, and slowly walked off the stage.

Just Gerald called for another centaur who led me to the archery range. It wasn't much of a range. It was just hay bales stacked up three high and three-deep. Three-deep was interesting because it spoke to the power of their bows. There was white material on them that looked like burlap but probably wasn't. The material was entirely white so I assumed the targets would be hung on them in the morning. After I checked to make sure the ground was relatively flat and even, and there were no hidden dips or obstacles that would screw up my range findings, I was satisfied and allowed them to lead me back to a small tent that was provided for me.

The inside of the tent was a pleasant surprise. There was a small coal fire already burning in a pit in the corner, and the smoke was almost non-existent. The tent was warm and there were comfortable blankets on the floor. There was a bucket of clear water and even a smaller cup for drinking. Beside the water was an assortment of cheese and fruits that looked heavenly. There wasn't any protein, but my supplies could supplement that. I had maybe ten hours until the shoot, so I carefully checked my bow and string; everything was perfectly tuned, and the pull was correct. I didn't have any target arrows but what I had would work. After checking everything over, I did some light stretching just to help me relax and laid down on the bed.

I didn't expect to sleep much, I never do, and I never do. I especially didn't expect to dream since I hadn't had a single dream since the accident, but apparently my expectations were not going to be considered. I lay down and fell asleep almost instantly.

I woke up with a start and looked around. I wasn't in the tent anymore. I was in a hospital room. The lights were way too bright, and everything was fuzzy, but somehow, I knew I was being operated on. I looked down and, yup, I could see my insides. Only they weren't. I mean they were mine, but they weren't insides. They looked clean and unspoiled and tough and hairy. Okay, gross. Things were moving inside me. Things I wanted to control but couldn't. While I was examining my guts, I saw a pair of hands, or paws—yeah, paws, that's it. They were holding a cleaver, a scalpel, and a set of my old Allen wrenches. I looked up at the things holding the instruments and they looked like giant Irish Wolf Hounds. Now if you haven't seen Irish Wolf Hounds in person, they are pretty giant to begin with. But these were at least ten feet tall and quite frankly looked more silly than scary with surgical masks fixed on their pointy ears. I started to ask them what was going on and I was back in the car.

Oh, heck no. I was *not* reliving this. Not even in a dream, and I'm pretty sure at this point I was dreaming. I was in the backseat and the car was warm. I was listening to Mama and Daddy prattle on about things like they did. I wanted to scream. I wanted to warn them. We were moments away from getting hit by the motorcycle. Motorcycle? That wasn't right.

I tried to close my eyes, but I couldn't. I stared intently

ahead and tried not to see the crash coming. Only in my dream now it wasn't a motorcycle. It was more like a deer driving a truck through the windshield. I tried to focus on that but then everything went fuzzy.

I was beside the road. Nothing hurt and everything should have. I did not want to look to the left because Mama and Daddy would be there, in the car, dead. But I did and they weren't. I mean, I looked left and the car was there. But Daddy wasn't. He was walking away, smoking a cigarette, which he thinks I don't know about, and talking to a ghost. Daddy never turned back as he walked away. I tried to call out and get him to not leave me, but I couldn't. Then I saw Mama climb out of the car, assisted by an honest-to-goodness angel, and walk in the other direction. I shut my eyes and began to cry.

I opened my eyes and I was back in a room. It looked like the waiting room in a hospital. I was sitting there while the dogs who operated on me argued with the vampire that I had fought to get this mission about who was going to eat me. I was trying to figure out why the dogs saved me just to eat me when Brother Damian walked in. He did not say a word, but everyone heard "Stop."

I woke up and shot straight to my feet. A knife was in my hand and my heart was pounding like I had run a marathon. I had been crying in my sleep and snot was running down my nose. That was not my best look. I know some girls can cry and look good. I am not one of them.

"Are you awake?" I heard from outside the tent. "The competition is to begin in thirty minutes and the Seer has requested a moment of your time beforehand."

"Give me five minutes to collect myself," I yelled at the tent. I only needed a minute or two to secure everything, but I definitely needed a few moments to regain my composure and eat some more fruit and cheese—and energy bars. I really did not feel like eating, but it beat potentially cramping during the shoot.

Five minutes later (give or take) I was as composed as I was going to be, so I left the tent and followed a centaur I hadn't met before to the Seer's tent. It wasn't much of a follow as her tent was only ten feet away but hey, it was the thought that counted.

I didn't see anywhere to knock on the large flap, so I just said, "Excuse me, ma'am," in my politest tone.

"Enter," she said, and I did.

Her tent was large, but it seemed to be even larger from the inside. There were furs laid about toward the back where I assumed that she lay down, if centaurs did that. There was what appeared to be a standing desk set at her height, and even some knickknacks here and there. All in all, it felt very homey and not at all like the lair of a powerful Seer.

"Did you sleep well?" she asked in a calm voice.

"I did not, ma'am," I replied. "I slept. I slept a lot for me. I even dreamed, and I can't remember the last time I did that. On a scale of one to suck, I would give my night a solid 'suck'."

She smiled. "I am sorry about that, child," she said although she did not seem all that sorry to me. "Some of that was my doing. I put you close to me so I could help you sleep and maybe help you find something out about yourself." She paused and seemed to be trying to find the right words. Finally, she began again. "There is much about you that you do not know. There is very little that I know about you, and even less that I feel I should share. I had hoped that I could help you begin to rediscover yourself. I would not have done this without your permission and knowledge, and a lot more training, if you had the time. However, one way or another you will be leaving us today. I did not feel right having such a damaged child leaving without at least trying to help."

"Okay, I guess. Um, thank you? Damaged? I'm confused."

"Good, then," she replied, responding only to the confusion. "That is an excellent start. One should never be too certain. Especially one such as you." With those cryptic remarks she led me out of her tent and to the archery range.

And, oh, goody. It looked like the word had spread about our little competition. There were at least twenty-five centaurs milling about and waiting. Oddly, all of them male. I was really beginning to wonder about that. Was this some special herd or were centaur women that rare? Or were the female centaurs not allowed to travel with the men? That thought irked me.

Good, Munchkin. Keep that in mind. Daddy always said that I shot my best when I was upset. Of course, he also that said that I was always upset so it was hard to tell. He never quite got used to raising a girl. He tried his best, and he meant well, it's just that boys really cannot understand girls. I guess when your only three emotions are hungry, horny, and beer, girls would be a ginormous mystery.

I walked up to what I supposed was the shooting line and waited. Just Gerald came trotting up. He looked very confident. The jerk. He bowed his head to the Seer and then looked at me and held out two fists. "Choose one," he said in an oddly ceremoniously tone. I chose the one on the left. He opened it and there was one pebble in it. He opened the other fist and there were two in it. "You shoot first, little human," he fairly sneered. Then he bowed again to the Seer, and said to her, "You may set the first spider."

"Wait, what?" I said. "Place a spider? What?"

For those of you who do not shoot archery, the spider is supposed to be the little cross, or "x" in the center of the target.

Just Gerald just shook his head at me and moved a couple of paces to the left. While he was doing so the Seer walked out to the first target.

"Are you ready, Warrior Munchkin?" she asked, and I drew my bow in response.

Centaurs were evidently really disciplined shots if she was willing to stand there, seemingly completely undisturbed while we shot. It bothered me somewhat that she was going to be downrange. That would never be allowed on *any* range back home. Maybe it was some sort of centaur bravery thing? Where they have to prove their bravery or something? But it seemed stupid and careless to me. *HEY! You're in a literal life-or-death tournament . . . remember? Focus, girl!*

Anyway, as I refocused, instead of showing proper fear of being shot, especially by someone she had never even seen hold a bow, she held out a glass bottle, unstopped it and held the rim to the target. She then removed it and stepped back quickly, which was somewhat of a relief. As she stepped back, I saw a tiny black spider in the center of the target streaking as fast as he could down and to the left.

Crap, I thought about how ready I wasn't for that, while my unconscious mind took over and shot the arrow. That was the good thing about shooting hundreds of arrows a day for a couple of years. I never had to think to shoot accurately. I simply released and watched the arrow fly at the moving spider. I missed it. I didn't really expect to hit it as fast as it was moving but I was only maybe six inches from it when it stopped moving. *Not bad, Munchkin,* I congratulated myself and turned to Just Gerald with a smile. "Your turn."

The running spider would bring luck into play, and I had just gotten very lucky. I was feeling optimistic, but of course, that couldn't last.

Just Gerald just looked at me and just walked right to where I was just standing and just raised his bow to show he was just ready. The jerk.

The Seer placed the glass again, presumably with a different spider, and stepped back. Just Gerald just waited. And he just waited some more while the spider raced for the edge. When it got to the edge it turned and went back toward the center. Just Gerald waited. It went toward the other edge and Just Gerald just waited some more. It appeared draw weight was not a problem as he his hold was solid as a stone. Just a few more seconds later the slider stopped in the lower left corner and Just Gerald just placed an arrow right through it.

"I believe round one is mine," he said, smiling.

Jerk.

Well double crap, Munchkin. You should have asked more questions. Ha! That never used to be my problem. Okay, one to nothing. Still four targets left. It could be worse. And no, I am not going to say it could be raining. Or it could be windy. I am not jinxing myself that much.

The second target (forty meters, if you are keeping track) went much better. This time I waited until the spider stopped moving and put an arrow through its little body. *Take that, Just Gerald*, I thought and then was quickly shut up as he did the same: He put his arrow into the middle of his little spider target as well.

The third target went the same. At the fourth, Just Gerald shot first. Must be some weird centaur rule. It did not matter. It went the same way. Just Gerald and I had put arrows into tiny spider bodies at sixty and one hundred meters. Now we were down only to the two hundred-meter target. Just Gerald shot first. It was a beautiful shot and I felt my heart fall.

Well, I guess I am going to be summarily executed, I thought as I turned to congratulate my opponent. The crowd was cheering and well they should. That shot was amazing. I would have had a hard time duplicating it, even if it would have mattered.

"Wait! Look!" came a cry from a centaur in the crowd.

We looked down the range and I could see the little spider running awkwardly away from the arrow. Just Gerald had just winged it! I had hope! I mean, not a lot of hope. I am the best shot I know and that is not being modest. I have proven it many times in many competitions, and that was before I got all my enhancements, but now I had to hit a spider at two hundred meters or lose my head. No pressure.

The Seer removed Just Gerald's arrow, placed the wounded spider in another container and placed a new glass against the target. I drew my bow. The glass was removed, and the spider took off straight down. I waited for it to stop. It didn't! It ran right off the bottom of the target. I was so screwed. I held my bow at the bottom of the target and hoped it would appear. Thirty seconds later, it hadn't. Another thirty, nothing. My arms weren't getting tired yet but shaking would start at some point, especially as nervous as I was getting. I was nearly to the point of conceding, I mean I would have conceded earlier if death wasn't involved, when I saw it emerge at the top right of the target. *Okay, Munchkin, now or never.* I released the arrow. My arrow hit the spider and, at that angle, went through the target and slammed into the ground a few yards behind it.

The Seer trotted down, grabbed my arrow and returned. She showed us the glass with the spider Just Gerald had injured.

"She hit the spider?" he asked. She nodded. "Do you have the arrow?"

She nodded again and handed it to him. Uh-oh. That arrow had flown into the ground. There was no chance that any tiny spider guts were going to be left on it. The Seer handed the arrow to Just Gerald and he examined it.

Then he looked at her, and asked, "And you are certain she killed the spider?"

"I am," came her solemn reply. "But I have no proof. Victory is yours."

"Bah," Just Gerald cursed, shaking his head. "There is no victory in this." He turned to me. "You shoot like a centaur, little warrior. I propose one more end. Winner to take all. You shoot first."

I did not have much choice, so I just nodded. I also said, "Thank you, Just Gerald. You are a true and worthy competitor." He did not respond. Instead, he turned to the crowd, and bellowed, "One more end! Touching arrows!"

One more end was obvious. An "end" is just what a round of arrows is called. But "touching arrows?" That sounded more like something boys would giggle about than it did an archery term.

"Shoot an arrow into the first target," he said to me. "Anywhere." I nodded and shot an arrow roughly into the center. Maybe not dead center because I did not aim for anything, but it was close. Just Gerald nodded and put an arrow close enough to mine to touch it. *Oh yeah. Oh, crap. So, this was touching arrows.* I drew and aimed much more carefully this time. My arrow landed close enough to his to make it wobble. He nodded. Good enough, I guess. He shot again and his arrow landed a good foot to the right of mine. What the heck? No way he missed by that much!

I looked at him and he just smiled. "I had two concerns about you, little warrior. I thought you human or Fae. While I do not know if you are, I do begin to doubt. The Seer," he said nodding to her, "vouches for you and I think that should have been good enough for me in the first place. My second concern was, quite simply, my own prejudice. I did not think you worthy to be in our woods." He looked at the Seer now, instead of me. "I know of my prejudices and I strive to be better." He turned back to me. "You shoot like a centaur. I would never have believed that to be true of any other race. You are calm and cool under pressure. You would have admitted defeat if your spider had not reappeared. I saw that in your eyes. There was no quit in you, but there was nobility in your defeat. I name you kin to my herd. You may call upon us at your need." He bowed surprisingly gracefully for half a horse and then turned to the crowd. "We have a new member of our herd! Let us celebrate tonight!"

Holy crap!

That night there was a lot of revelry, wine to be drunk, food to be eaten, and more centaurs than I thought were here to meet and get to know me as the newest member of the herd. It was fun and wonderful and inclusive and more like family than anything I had felt since the accident. It would have been awesome, but I needed to leave, and soon.

Sometime after midnight I made my way back to my tent and was just entering when I heard the Seer call out from inside her tent. "Rest well, child. I hope you find that which you are searching. I think we will meet again."

With those mysterious words, I lay down for a couple of hours' of (thankfully!) dreamless sleep. I was up early the next morning and headed east. I saw only one centaur as I left. Just Gerald was up to say goodbye.

"So long, little Warrior Munchkin," he said with a smile. "Good hunting to you."

"Thank you, Gerald," I said, feeling touched.

"Oh no," he replied. "You call me 'Just Gerald.' I find I like that." He smiled and trotted away.

15
BULLOPOLIS

Okay. According to the centaurs, I had a hard day's trot to get to the edge of their forest and into the land of the Bull King. They did not know for certain how long it would take after that. They believed I would have to pass through a large city to get there. Since they didn't know its name, I dubbed it Bullopolis. Then presumably I just had to get through a maze, and I could get to the castle proper. Or, get through the castle proper and I could get to the maze. They weren't sure.

I was assuming I would have to go through the castle to get to the maze. The whole "maze first thing" didn't make sense to me since I assumed groceries had to be delivered to the castle. No way the farmers of Bullopolis negotiated a maze every day to deliver fresh fruits and vegetables.

The centaurs also told me with certainty that I would see no intelligent or dangerous life until I was near the forest edge. They ruled the forest with an iron fist, and with one notable exception, non-centaurs did not enter the woods. Predators such as bears and wolves had been eliminated years ago so that the deer and rabbit population would thrive for them to hunt. There may be the occasional fox, but I've yet to meet a normal fox I couldn't take in a fair fight. I wasn't going to let my guard down, but it did appear I could breathe a little easier today. Well, except for the hard trotting, of course.

Well, long story short, after nearly half a day trotting as quickly as I could through a calm and welcoming forest, I saw the end of it. It was as abrupt as it had been on its westerly front. There were trees everywhere and then they stopped. I reached the edge, looked out at the bright sun I hadn't seen clearly for a while through the trees, and decided to wait for a few minutes to catch my breath.

My energy bar stash was starting to get decidedly too low. I had a large number of berries and nuts I had foraged along the way, but I was going to have to ration my bars if I did not find more protein soon. At least I could start rationing my pills as the Seer had said that they were more for energy than health. Maybe it was silly to trust her more than the people who had trained me, but the things she said had the echo of truth, and I no longer believed in my trainers' version of the facts. That was heartbreaking, but something I would have to deal with later, over ice cream. You know, like when I didn't have kids to save or a ridiculous timeline that I was no longer even certain about.

Thanks again, Mobius.

So, after a couple of minutes thinking dark thoughts, I set off toward the rising sun. I know that sounds mystical and promising and all, but it was sort of a pain squinting all the time. My eyes handled brightness fairly well, much better than a standard human, but I still preferred a peaceful, overcast day.

The east side of the forest seemed very similar to the west side, sans inept robbers, and I walked for a few hours through a pleasant, rolling grassland interspersed with farms and ranches. It took me a while before I noticed the odd difference between ranches here and back at home; there were no cattle. I guess that made sense being the home of the Bull King and all that, but I was going to miss a juicy steak at the next inn I stopped in. If, of course, I ever got to one.

Eventually, I had found a smaller road which led to a larger one which led to a very well-traveled one, so I had to assume I was getting close. And I was! Around midday I topped a small hill and saw Bullopolis below me. It was much larger than the hamlet, Hamlet, I was in earlier. It was nowhere near as large as Chicago, or even South Bend for that matter, but compared to the lack of civilization I had been walking through recently, it looked like a metropolis. Buildings stretched along at least three major streets and I counted them to be at least thirty-deep.

They went all the way to the base of a mountain.

The mountain itself was not extremely tall and did not look overly daunting. It appeared to have more of a gradual slope than sharp, jagged inclines, and was covered with the same trees as in the forest I had recently visited. I did not see any clear paths up it but that stood to reason with the tree cover. If you are curious as to why I was so interested in the mountain, and even if you aren't, it is because at the very top of the mountain sat a castle. I assumed that was my ultimate destination.

The castle looked like I expected a castle to look. It was made of stone, or maybe rock, with a solid wall surrounding it that enclosed more buildings, and a large, gated entrance. We'd never lived in a gated community when I was growing up because Daddy always said that gated communities had too many rules and if they wanted to paint the damn house pink and yellow, he damned well would. I always thought that was odd because we lived in a two-story white house with a well-maintained lawn. I guess it was more the thought of restrictions than the actual ones that he didn't like. Sometimes my Dad was weird.

Exciting thoughts like that and others kept me entertained as I walked the rest of the way into Bullopolis, which I learned was actually named Creter, at least according to the sign just outside of town. Okay, I hadn't been in any real cities for a while and my first impression of Bullopolis was that it was a bit overwhelming. The first thing that hit me was the smell. There was horse manure, but I never minded that. For those of you that don't know, horse manure actually smells kind of sweet, and like nature.

It was the smell of garbage, and sewage running in the street, and unwashed people all mixed with vague smells that I didn't want to parse out that almost brought tears to my eyes and made me want to sneeze. In fact, the smell was so bad I almost missed that a large portion of the population was human. I guess I sort of figured Bullopolis, sorry, Creter, would be full of elves and magically clean and smell good. Ugh, guess not.

Anyway, I quickly found an inn cleverly named "INN" and stepped through the swinging doors. Cool. Just like the old west. I looked around and it was similar to the last inn I was in, only larger. There was a large fireplace in the center big enough to roast an entire deer. I would have thought cow, but, you know, place run by a bull. There were two smaller fireplaces with stewpots cooking on either side of it. I could smell fresh bread baking even over the vague, sad smell all these places seemed to have. There were twenty small tables that could hold five people if you packed them in. There was also a stage area where a bard, or maybe a three-person band could perform. Off to the right was an open doorway where I assumed the food and drink would come from. Off to the left was a large bar area where a few hardy souls were industriously day-drinking their cares away. Behind them was a stairway.

Well, this seemed like a good place to start. Only seven of the tables were occupied and no one at them looked particularly dangerous, or even interesting. I was looking for knowledge and these people either had the look of persons who had come in from the field to sell stuff and were getting busy laying in a full belly before proceeding back out, or people who drank here until it was time to find a place to sleep until they could drink here again.

I didn't attract as much attention as I had feared, which was nice, so I made my way to a table where I could see the entire establishment, sat down with my back to the wall, and almost sighed with relief as I took a load off my weary feet. Now, I rarely get tired, or even really sore, but I had been walking for a long while, and it was nice to just not be moving for a moment. With that happy thought, I sat and waited to be waited on.

I was seated less than two minutes when a serving girl approached me. She could have been the twin of the one who served me at the last inn. That thought made me smile and she seemed put at ease by my expression.

"I'll have a large slice of that venison cooking in the fireplace, a bowl of each of whatever is in the stewpots, bread, and water, if it's clean. I'll also want a bed for a couple of hours if the rooms are clean." I held the smile in place. That isn't easy for me. I am a teenager and "frown" is more my default setting, but I was trying out something new.

"We have our own well," she responded, "so the water is clean and pure. Stew in both pots so do you want two bowls? Is someone joining you?"

"No," I replied, my face beginning to hurt from all the smiling. "Just a large bowl, instead of two, then. About that room?"

"Oh, yes, the rooms are clean," she said, standing straighter and with obvious pride. "This is my father's inn and it is very respectable. Not like the other ones around here." She hesitated for long enough to make me wonder if I'd lost her before continuing. "That'll be two silvers."

"Here," I said, reaching into my pouch and coming out with a gold piece. "How much will this get me?"

She looked shocked at my display of wealth. "Why, that would get you lunch, dinner, a room for the night, and since you are not drinking wine, I am thinking it would do all of that again for at least a month," she claimed with something akin to awe in her voice.

Well, I had several of those and I wasn't counting on taking a lot back with me. "Tell you what. I am not planning on staying all that long. You keep me in food until I am stuffed, maybe bring me a bottle of wine if I am joined by someone wishing to drink, make sure my bed is clean, my breakfast is hot if I'm here that long, and the coin is yours." I hesitated because this was the one thing I really needed. "Oh, yeah," I said as if it had just occurred to me, "you warn me if anyone I do not want to deal with comes in, and if someone with knowledge of the castle up there shows up, send them my way." I handed her the coin. Maybe I should rob robbers more often. It certainly made spending evidently large sums of money relatively easy.

She curtsied once, grabbed the coin, and scurried toward the kitchen. I pretended not to see her bite the coin or put it into the front of her dress rather than a pocket or someplace where she might need to account for it. She was back less than five minutes later with what appeared to be a quarter of a small deer, a bowl of stew that looked like it might double for a hot tub, an entire loaf of bread, and a pitcher of water.

"Miss," she said with obvious friendship—at least friendship of gold, "I would say that there will probably not be any merchants returning from the castle until supper or after. If you like I can show you to a room after you eat, and you can freshen up and walk about the town."

"Thank you," I said.

There was no chance I was leaving my stuff in a room while I wandered about, but I could use it to soak and clean all my clothes, polish and check my blades, and take a sponge bath. It's funny. I've read many fantasy books written by boys and they never seem to mention smelling awful after a few days on the road or having to clean their undies. I am hoping that was just glossing over and not boys being truly gross.

"Do you happen to have a bath?"

"We do," she said, mentally counting that total away from her gold.

"Make sure it is hot and very private," I said, handing her a couple of copper coins. "Also, please have a smaller one by it so I can wash my clothes as well."

She brightened—a lot—with the addition of the copper coins and went to make my bath ready. I dug into the meat, which was stupid good, smoked to perfection, fat dripping off it, and spiced lightly, but well. After that I turned to the stew and bread, both of which were excellent.

Once, when I was a little girl my family took a trip to France. I remember how everywhere we ate the food was amazing. This reminded me of Paris. Not that the food tasted the same, but in the fact the food wasn't processed to the point you weren't certain what you were eating. Anyway, twenty or so minutes later I was sitting back satisfied and with a distended stomach when the girl returned to let me know my bath was ready.

"Excellent," I responded with a true smile this time. "Show me the way. Also, save this table for me. I find I like its view of the inn."

I soaked in the bath until the water, which was near boiling to start, had turned room temperature. Then I turned my attention to getting my clothing as clean and stink-free as possible. I would be damp for a couple of hours, but that was a small price to pay to smell decent again. After that I made my way to my room, cleaned, checked, and/or honed everything that needed cleaning, checking, and/or honing, and lay down for a couple of hours. I didn't really want to sleep, I wanted to be finding out information and moving on as quickly as possible. I guessed I was rapidly running out of time but stretching out on a relatively soft and very clean bed felt wonderful, and my best chance to find information without attracting unwanted attention would most likely soon be arriving to eat.

Two hours later, I was back and sitting at my table which the serving girl had saved for me. I sat, ordered bread, honey, and water, and waited for someone to walk in with the information I needed. A couple hours spent people-watching, getting bored, getting restless, fretting about lost time, reconsidering life choices, etc., later, a man who was obviously a relatively well-off merchant walked in.

I studied him as he approached. He was really old, maybe forty, with thinning hair and a slight paunch he was trying to hide. His clothes were more colorful than those of the other town folks' I'd seen, and of a better cut. His skin was weathered by the sun and his formerly dark hair was shot through with the beginnings of gray. He gave me the standard smile older men give younger women. The look that says they think they are still young enough to be interesting and that they know more than you do.

If women had half the self-esteem of even the ugliest male, we would easily own the world. After all, even at my age I'd begun to notice that males had only three going concerns: food, alcohol, and sex. They could provide all of those things for themselves but seemed to be desperately looking for a woman to do it for them—especially the sex part.

Mama used to tell me providing that part for the right man was a lot of fun, but I would have to get used to just how much time they spent trying to get it. Thinking of that gave me two thoughts (1) ewwe and (b) gross. Thinking about parents in that way was an endless rabbit hole of icky.

I suppressed all of this, stood with my hand out, and gave him the smile teenaged girls give older men. The one that says,

"Aren't you cute?"

He shook my hand a tad wimpily and took a seat. "Well, young miss . . . I assume young? One can never tell these days what with spells, mixed-heritage, and so on. How may I be of assistance?" He smiled proudly and continued in an overly friendly voice, "I am Master Baden, the finest purveyor of gems, baubles, and lovelies in the land."

"I'm sorry," I said in all seriousness, "did you just say your name was Master Bador?"

"Baden, young miss," he said with a smile that told me that he actually hadn't heard that one before, or just didn't get it. "Now how may I be of assistance?" I fought back a smile that no teenage boy could have hidden. Did he really think Baden was any better than Bador?

"Well," I said, "as nice as your merchandise sounds," it didn't really, he looked moderately prosperous but nowhere near what I'd think of when I thought of as "finest," "I am in need of information, and willing to pay."

"Ah, information," he said, trying to sound wise, "the coin of the wise person. What say we start with a nice bottle of wine and we can discuss my fee after I hear what you need."

I nodded. "That sounds nice." If this idiot thought that he could drink me into a better deal or, ugh, something more, he was in for a rough night. My metabolism meant I'd probably start sloshing and turn into a giant grape before I'd even get a buzz from wine.

I ordered wine, bread, and cheese before continuing. "I am not from around here. I long to see the castle and am wondering how visitors are treated there."

He looked at me for a long moment and took a huge gulp of wine, not seeming even to taste it. "I think not, miss," he said with a frown. "You are well-armed, hold yourself with the confidence of an equal, and are seeking information that could get me into a great deal of trouble. I see no upside to giving you this information. Good day." He started to rise.

"A moment, good sir," I said, holding out a gold coin I had palmed. "You said no upside for you. Perhaps I can reward you in the love of merchants everywhere. But I guess if you have made up your mind, I can always find another person to give me some harmless information."

"May I?" he asked, trying to feign disinterest but holding out his hand for the coin with an air of undisguised greed.

I gave it to him to examine and he put it in his pouch. If we didn't come to an agreement about information, we were definitely going to have a serious discussion about that coin.

"Perhaps if you had three more to match this, we could do business."

I gave him the famous teenage girl look of haughty derision.

"Three? Don't be silly, good sir," I said, changing my look to a smile. "I might have one more. Maybe. If the information is all that I need."

He smiled like a shark getting ready to feed, or a teenage boy at an all-you-can-eat buffet. "One more will not do. I'm thinking I would be needing to take a long trip north or south and be there long before you do whatever it is you are doing. And for the record, I don't want to know. Three is cutting you a bargain because you paid for drinks and have been such a pleasant companion."

"Well," I said, pretending to be sad, "it seems you have a problem, good sir. At least twenty people have seen you talking to me. At this point I'd say you are going to be blamed." I paused for effect. "Now, if I was successful, or even if I was not apprehended—assuming, of course, I was doing something that could cause one to be apprehended—then there is no way your name would come up, Master Baden."

"I see," he said, no longer seeming happy at all. "It seems you have me at a disadvantage. Two more coins, of gold, and I will share all I know."

"One and one only. And that is only if I deem the information worthy of such a large sum." I sat there with a confident look on my face.

I was nowhere near confident. I only had one more gold coin

and I doubted there would be some other bandits waiting around to donate more funds.

He hesitated and I took the other gold piece out and placed it on the table in front of him. Who says you can't learn anything watching reality TV? Everyone knows if you just put the money in front of someone, they have to take it. And, long story short, he did.

"Very well, young miss," he said, pocketing the second gold piece. I looked meaningfully at the pocket where he placed it. He was giving both of them back if I didn't get what I needed.

He glanced around the room, saw no one obviously listening to us and no one close enough to do so effectively, before lowering his voice conspiratorially and continuing. "I am going to be making some assumptions here. Just nod your head if I am correct." I nodded. "You want to get to the castle as quickly as possible." Nod. "You would like to avoid customs, inspections, guards." Nod. "You would prefer a quiet entrance." Nod. "You don't mind taking a couple of reasonable chances." Nod. "You can fight." Nod. "You are going alone, or a very small group." Nod.

He hesitated for a few moments by taking a swig of wine and calling for another bottle. "I don't like this," he said, shaking his head. "Adventurer you may be, but you still have the innocent look of a little girl. I have one myself, you know?"

I nodded. I doubted it. At least I doubted he had one he took care of in any meaningful way. There is a difference between being a donor and being a father, and he didn't look like the type of person who'd know that . . . at least until he needed something from her.

"Okay," he continued, "the main road is probably out. It's a straight shot, maybe six to seven hours straight up the mountain. However, there are three checkpoints along the way stationed at areas where draft animals can rest. Also, they are stationed in areas where it would be very difficult to pass around them. The guards there, like most places, aren't really sharp or honest. A few bribes might get you through. A young miss traveling by herself up to that castle, or even in a small group couldn't help but cause a little stir, though. You know of the castle's reputation?"

I shook my head, and he continued, "There are rumors about missing children that are not pleasant." He paused for a moment while he remembered how unpleasant those rumors must be and then continued, "Once you get into the castle grounds people will just think they haven't seen you before. Hopefully. But getting there would be an issue."

"So far you haven't given me much for my money other than telling me what I cannot do," I said.

"Patience, young miss, patience. There is another way. Only

one. The mountain is much more sheer than she appears, and the rocks are too loose for climbing." He smiled. "Unless you have a lot more of those gold pieces lying around?" I shook my head. "Well, then, it is extremely dangerous. There is a path that winds around the mountain. The king's guards do not patrol it. They want people on the main road. If you leave the main roads there are bandits at every turn if you believe the rumors. How that many bandits would make a living all lined up in a row like that is anyone's guess, but that is the tale. I've never gone that way. I don't know anyone who has and actually made it to the castle. Rumor is the journey's three days or so. Good enough?"

I thought about it for a minute, going over possibilities in my mind. Three days was probably at least a day too long, but I can move a lot faster than most people. Besides, what choice did I have?

"How do I find this path?"

"The main road out of town reaches the mountain after less than an hour's walk. Start up the mountain for twenty minutes or so. You will see a gnarled old tree that died years ago. Turn right at that tree and start walking. That is the path. Supposedly. As I said, I do not know of anyone who actually made it that way. One last thing, and I know this sounds odd: I once met a traveler who claims he met a crippled person who tried it. He said the person was delirious and just kept saying 'Sleep is either too long or too short.' I have no idea what that means or if it is really true." He paused, looking at me with a question. When I did not respond because I didn't know what he was asking, he frowned and said, "Are we good? Is the transaction complete?"

"Yes. You may keep the gold." I smiled. "One condition, though. If you are lying to me, or tell anyone what I might be planning, I will be back for that gold. I'm sure neither of us want that."

He nodded, gulped the last of his wine, and bid me good luck before heading out, presumably either to care for his merchandise, or to rat me out.

16
THE MOUNTAIN

So, after too little sleep, I woke up relatively refreshed but groggy. I know, I know, I say too little sleep a lot. But hey, teenager here! And you try going through what I have been going through, while catching only one- or two-hours' sleep at a time. I had only gotten one full night rest since my journey began, and that rest was one big nightmare.

Anyway, I dressed, checked my equipment again because you can never be too careful, ate a hearty breakfast, and headed for the castle. Any luck and this might finally soon be over. I needed to keep more kids from dying. Honestly? I was also really looking forward to a hot shower and a rare steak. And chocolate, oh, my, yes, chocolate, and pie, and maybe even a Pop-Tart or two. Non-frosted, of course. I am not a barbarian.

With a smile on my face and a song in my heart—"This is Me," if you're curious—I headed for the outskirts of town and, would you believe it? Wow! A Starbucks. I guess one world really is not enough for them. I stopped in and ordered a Double Chocolatey Chip Frappuccino with a triple shot of espresso for later, and swooped up all the energy bars they had. A short walk after and I was on the mountain and looking for an old tree.

The tree was an easy find and I took a right turn. Good, first hurdle passed. Now just to head straight until I found a road. I didn't, of course, find a road right away. I walked as quickly as I could without risking a broken ankle through scrub brush and densely packed trees, hoping that I was still going in the right direction until I spotted a clearing about ten feet ahead.

This was the first clearing I'd seen since starting out and I figured it didn't bode well. I think I figured that because there was a giant in the clearing. Not a literal one, but a really big dude. He was maybe eight feet tall and really, really thick. He looked vaguely like Andre the Giant in stature but with more muscle and hair. Definitely more hair. Gross. He wore old, weathered, leather armor with studs sewn in.

Oh, yeah. He was also a cyclops. A cyclops with a very, very large club that looked like it was wrapped in bronze. Maybe I should have led with that.

"Give me all of your belongings and you may pass," came a voice so deep I could swear I felt it.

"Well met, good sir," I said, stalling for time and looking for a weakness. No time to get my bow out so I worried I'd have to fight this guy. That was troubling because, you know, huge, and the club that was longer and probably weighed more than me. He was also holding it like I'd hold a Wiffle ball bat. This could suck.

"And how shall I address you, sir?" I asked, still searching for any advantage.

"I am called Periphetes. Now," he said, hefting his giant club in one hand and bouncing it in the other, "leave your belongings and you may pass."

I smiled. "Otherwise I shall not pass? No? LOTR? Gandalf? Nothing? Oh, well, hey, I'd like to help you out here. I really would. But you see, I need my stuff. Maybe we can come to an arrangement? Shoot dice or something?"

"Do not seek to distract me, little girl, and keep your hand from that bag," he said, seeing that I was reaching for my bow. "You can just leave the whole bag." I stopped trying to get out my bow and motioned for him to continue. "I have no interest in games, only gold. You have nothing that I want other than that, girl. Simply give me what I wish, or I will be forced to take it from you," he said while hefting the club into a more menacing position.

Okay, now I was a little peeved. "What do you think this is, prom night? Give you what you want? And what is this 'girl' crap? Girls are at least the equal of boys. You, sir, are a chauvinist." I was really working myself up. Not the best position to begin a fight but the whole "girl" thing really set me off.

"I'll tell you what, counteroffer," I said, drawing a dagger in each hand. "How about you step off the road, let me pass, and I don't carve you into little bitty, Hairy Giant parts?"

He started to laugh, and I came forward much quicker than anyone his size should be able to counter. I shifted right and then left and noticed he didn't move laterally very well. That was my edge. His right leg was not working properly. Cool! I faked left and back to the right, counting on his lack of balance, and went in for a stab to that leg, followed by one to the gut.

Um. At least that was the plan. What actually happened was

a giant bronze club slammed into me and knocked me a good ten feet farther to the right. It probably would have been much farther if a handy tree hadn't stopped my momentum by allowing me to crash fully into it. Ouch. As I slid down the tree, I immediately noticed three things. One, my left arm was broken, b, I had at least three ribs that were either broken or seriously wanted to be, and 3, there was now a giant and a half walking fuzzily toward me. That last part was probably the concussion talking. Evidently, the handy tree had stopped my momentum head-first.

Well, stuff just got real. *I heal really fast,* I told myself as I pressed my broken arm into my broken ribs. They shifted back into place which allowed me to breathe . . . some. I mean, they only hurt when I breathed and I couldn't take any deep breaths, but they hurt less than they did a second or so ago. Or maybe my arm just hurt worse. It was hard to tell. My arm would knit itself quickly but not fast enough to help me live through this fight. No need to worry about it, then, especially because I noticed my shoulder was not in its socket.

"People have come at my bad leg for more years than you've been alive, little girl," he said while closing the distance between us. "One last chance, give me your belongings and I'll let you wander down the path to die." He raised his club for the coup de Munchkin.

The knife I had in my right hand was basically worthless at this point, so I grabbed it by the point with my left hand and threw it cross-body at his face. For the record, I had no hope of doing any real damage. And sadly, I was right. The knife hit him a foot below where I aimed and pommel first. What it did do was give me a precious half second. I used that half second, and the momentum of the knife throw to keep rolling, barely getting out of the way of the club that went smashing down where I had been sitting.

I pushed to my feet and mostly ignored the anguish of rolling across a broken arm and badly bruised ribs and stepped back a couple of steps. At least there was only one of him now and he was mostly not blurry. Of course, I was mostly dead, so I figured best case, he was still winning.

He swung the club backhanded at me and I barely jumped back out of the way. Even landing from my jump caused so much pain in my arm I felt tears come to my eyes. And just to put the icing on the cake, he swung again almost as fast and I barely dodged again. He was swinging that giant club like it weighed nothing. He didn't even have the courtesy to be breathing hard.

Okay, plan c. I dodged another swing that would easily have made me a Munchkin pancake and feinted at his bad leg. He did as I expected this time and came down to block. I kicked him as hard as I could on the inside knee of his good leg. Ouch! Not him, me. I'm not sure if I broke my shin or just bruised it enough that it really didn't matter. I'd broken concrete blocks with kicks like that. He was solid.

"Call it a draw?" I asked hopefully.

He didn't bother to respond, just took a couple of steps toward me. He wasn't as steady on either leg now, so I knew that I had at least bruised the giant beast. Yay for me! Now what? Oh, yeah, here's an idea: Duck the massive club swinging at your head and then step back as it comes at me again.

Crap. I had to end this soon before he ended it for me. I didn't have a sling and a rock like David. I couldn't strangle him with my broken arm like that other hero, you know, the one in the red suit, so I did the only thing I could think of. I charged inside of his next swing and let his momentum pin me against his chest. Then I slid down between his legs and stabbed as hard as I could straight up into his taint. He let out a howl that a bull moose would be proud of and slammed his legs together.

Unfortunately, for me I was still between them and if my arm wasn't already broken his legs coming together would certainly have done the job. He started to drop to his knees, and I kicked him with everything I had in his belly. This caused him to fall back enough that he at least missed my face. Thank all that is holy for that.

While he was busy pulling my knife out, I grabbed another one while moving to my feet and literally dove at him and stabbed him in the eye. His stinking skull was so thick the knife took out his eye but did not penetrate far enough. Fortunately, he wasn't moving as fast as I was now, so I had enough time to ram my fist down on the hilt and drive the knife into his brain. "I win," I said and then rolled off of him and passed out.

I wasn't out long. My best guess is fifteen minutes or so. It would have been blissfully longer, but I turned a little and had a nightmare that some giant had broken my arm. Oh, yeah, that wasn't a dream. I had a broken arm, a dislocated shoulder, a shin that didn't seem to be broken but was probably a wonderful shade of purple, an eye that I thought was swollen shut but was just closed with dried blood, a headache that couldn't be measured on a normal scale, and more bruises than clear skin.

Okay. This was going to suck. A lot. And I mean whole new levels of suck. The first thing I did was stumble over to the nearest tree, take a huge breath, and slam my shoulder into it to get it back into the socket. As the pain hit and I slumped to the ground I realized I hadn't hit it hard enough and had to do it all over again.

After that, and a short cry, I strapped my hand to a thick branch and pulled until I got far enough that my bone was mostly back in place. As the pain slowly receded from that I realized I still had a rib almost poking through my skin, so I pressed it back into place. I figured I would be completely healed in no more than a few hours, but I didn't want to stay here that long. I didn't know if this guy had friends, or accomplices, or arms suppliers, but I was in no shape to find out.

I scoured the camp for food and found almost none. In fact, I found almost nothing at all that was usable except for a heavy purse and a couple of scraps of jerky that were too far gone to eat safely. What did this guy eat? Anyway, not my major problem. Time to hit the road. Fortunately, there was a path leading out. When you aren't sure which way to go, a path seems to be the best, if not safest option.

About an hour later the trail started to disappear so I just kept heading roughly straight. The trees were packed tighter together than in the Centaur Woods and the underbrush seemed determined to tangle my feet and branches scratched my face and hands at every opportunity. It was exhausting and I was bone-tired, sweaty—which is odd for me—my muscles ached so much a three-day hot tub soak followed by a two-day nap seemed like the only cure, and I was not healing nearly as fast as I thought I would. It seems energy bars and endlessly slogging along while every inch of me ached was not a cure-all for beaten Munchkins. I was stumbling and drained. I was also seriously considering a nap, or at least sitting under a tree and crying for a few minutes, when I saw a cabin only a few yards away.

Man, I must be tired for an entire cabin to sneak up on me. Anyway, I stumbled to it and knocked on the door.

17

CABIN IN THE WOODS

A kindly looking man opened the door with a smile and bade me to enter. He was really, really old, like fifty or something. He looked completely harmless. His hair was white and balding. His clothes were comfortable-looking, and I did not see a weapon concealed anywhere. His teeth were yellow and there was just the hint of needing a morning shave.

"Come in. Come in, young miss," he said in a very friendly voice. "You look all tired and done in. My goodness, did you fall down a hill or something? You're bruised from head to toe. The path here can do that to you. Tell me, can you possibly be as tired as you seem?"

His eyes were a deep blue and looking at them seemed to make me even more tired. I took a second to glance around for threats. It seemed like a very typical small cabin in the woods. There was a solid table and chairs in the middle of the room, a fireplace toward the back, a cabinet that was closed, and some cooking pots. There were two doors, one to either side of the fireplace which I assumed led to a bedroom and either a pantry or a washroom.

"I want to hear all about your journey, young traveler, but first, you look exhausted, you must rest."

He was right. Oh, goodness, was I tired. I could barely keep my eyes open as he led me to a small room to the left of the fireplace. The only things in it were two beds, a nightstand, and a small light burning on it. Two beds seemed very odd. What was even odder was one bed was way too long and one bed was too short. It reminded me of Goldilocks, but that didn't seem quite right. Something was off here, but I was too tired and sore to care.

"Choose a bed, little one," he said with a kind smile.

I was thinking it over when it suddenly occurred to me. Classical education strikes again! "Wait a second," I said, fighting hard to keep my eyes open. "I need to get something out of my bag first."

I reached in and took out the triple espresso I was saving for tomorrow's wake-up, grabbed it, and downed it in one swallow. Yuck! Cold espresso is not my thing, but even drinking it gave me the psychological boost that I needed to start waking up.

"Choose a bed, huh?" I said, thinking it over. "I have a counteroffer for you. How about this? Now listen to me carefully and think through my answer." I hesitated. "No."

"No, what?" he asked, confused. "You must choose a bed."

"Your name wouldn't happen to be Procrustes, would it?" I went on, not waiting for a reply. I could see in his face that I was right. "Well, Mr. Procrustes, I have no interest in fitting a bed. I just drank a LOT of caffeine. Gross and cold caffeine, but caffeine all the same. So, I'm not very tired at the moment.

What I am, is angry and exhausted." I thought about that for a second. "Which is totally different from being tired." Man, I was tired. I wasn't making sense even to me. "Now I will give you a choice. We can find some rope around here and I can tie you up so I can sleep in peace and you can enjoy a pain-free evening, or we can do things the hard way. Frankly, I'm too tired to argue anymore but not too tired to kick your old butt, so you make the call."

He looked stunned by my little speech and was so taken aback he didn't even think that the reason I was approaching him while speaking was to clock him in his stupid jaw with the hilt of the dagger I had palmed. He went down like a stone, or maybe like I'd wanted to when the giant clocked me, so it ended our debate before it really got started.

Fifteen minutes later, I'd thoroughly searched him for weapons—he didn't have any—then hog-tied and shoved him into the smaller bed, which I also tied him to. The bed was short enough that his legs hung off the end. But fortunately for him, I wasn't him, so he wouldn't be getting an "adjustment."

Instead, I also gagged him in case he snored, and searched the house. There was enough water for a complete cleansing for me and to get most of the stains, and stink, out of my clothing. I even found some stew fixings and hung them in a pot in the fireplace. All that done, I staggered to the larger bed and collapsed. The caffeine had worn out about two minutes after I drank it and I was running on fumes. Sleep came fast and deep.

After not enough sleep, maybe two hours, I awoke feeling much more refreshed than I thought I would. I was still sore, but my arm was usable, and while my shoulder clicked when I stretched it, it was long on the way toward being healed. I figured I'd be back to full fighting strength in a couple more hours. I ate most of the stew I had simmering and sat back with a contented sigh.

"Now, what am I going to do about you?" I called into the bedroom while I mopped up the last of the stew with some reasonably fresh bread.

"Oh, well, no help for it I guess," I said, and I grabbed an ax I found in the pantry and headed back into the room. I could see the terror in his eyes. "You have a very bad reputation, you know. Fitting poor travelers to your beds. It's really sick, you know?" I took the coverings off the bed I slept in and went about chopping it into two pieces. Then I cut him loose and rolled him off his bed and did the same to the bed where he was lying.

"Now," I said, "it seems you have two choices. I just made you adjustable beds. You can give me your word that you'll fit these newly adjustable beds to travelers, and not the reverse, or I can go ahead right now and adjust you to the fit into a small chair." I cut off his gag. "Choose."

Procrustes agreed not to adjust any more travelers, not that I trusted him, but I figured I'd killed enough people. Or *maybe* had killed enough people. The memory of what happened earlier with Periphetes was going to weigh heavily on my soul. I hoped to never do that again.

I felt the tears come but squashed them for now. There'd be time enough for that on the road. Besides, this was the land of myths. He'd probably be back, and it wasn't like he gave me a choice, or was last person I'd have to fight. For a land with the pleasant and peaceful name of Faerie, there sure seemed to be a lot of danger everywhere.

As I left Procrustes' house, he smiled a sad smile and waved me out the door.

Outside the cabin was the start of a narrow path. Oh, good, I was on my way. That cheery thought sped me on my way for a couple more hours of walking mostly uphill and wondering why I wasn't healing as fast as normal.

The path wound around and up the mountain and I felt as if I was making good progress. It was still too narrow to effectively carry my bow. I tried, and it kept snagging no matter how I carried it, so I kept my eyes and ears open for any surprises, and my bow in my bag.

I needn't have bothered. As I said, it was a couple hours later when I spotted another clearing a few feet in the distance. "Oh drat," I whispered to myself. "This can't be good."

18
WRESTLING WITH PROBLEMS

Sadly, I was right again. Sitting on a stump on the left side of a clearing was a man wearing nothing but ripped shorts. He was huge. Not like the last guy. This guy was built more like Brock Lesner's big brother. And I mean *really* big brother. I'm guessing close to four hundred pounds and none of it was fat. His hair was short, curly, and blond. He turned his head toward me, which surprised me because I didn't think he had a neck. His eyes were a bright blue. He smiled at me and his teeth were bright and even.

When he spoke it sounded like he was gargling rocks. "Well met, young miss. Come, join me," he said, motioning to another stump a few feet to his right.

Politeness rarely hurt anyone, so I walked over and sat facing him. "Well met, good sir."

"Tell me, young miss, what brings you here on this fine day?"

"Munchkin."

He looked confused. "Munchkin brings you here? What or who, pray tell, is Munchkin?"

"I am. You may call me Munchkin."

"Well, then, Miss Munchkin, what brings you here?"

"Merely passing through. I am on my way to the castle at the top of the hill."

He thought for a moment. "Ah, I see. Well, we may have an

issue."

"Pray tell, what issue?" I replied while reaching for a dagger, hopefully unobtrusively.

"Well, maybe not so much an issue but an opportunity. You need information. I need money. I am, you see, a bandit."

"I see," I said, seeing. "And you wish all my money?" I pretended to think for a moment. "How about this? I give you some money, you give me the information you think I need, and we part as friends?"

"Sadly, no," he said, actually seeming to sound sad. "You see, I am a bandit. I am afraid I need all your money, and your weapons, and anything else of value you may have."

I jumped off the stool and out of easy reach for him while producing the dagger I'd palmed and another I drew when I landed. "Counteroffer, I cut you into progressively smaller pieces until you give me the information I need, or I just walk away, and we part as neutral acquaintances?"

He shook his giant head. "Sadly, again no. I'll have to counter with option c. You see, get it, see? Option c? No? Never mind. You see, you'll either leave here on the correct path to the castle, or you'll wander these mountains for days through progressively worse and worse terrain. You cannot torture the information out of me, and even if you could, you'd never be able to trust it. So here is my counter to yours: We have a wrestling match, to the death. You win, you go free with all your money and directions. I win, you never leave here, and I get all your possessions."

I frowned. "That appears to be a no-win for me. You win the wrestling match and I am obviously never getting to the castle. I win and you're dead. I find it hard to believe that you can tell me which way to go if you are dead."

He thought about that for a moment. I guess no one had ever challenged his logic before. Suddenly, he brightened. "I concede your point and I think I have a workable solution. You place all your weapons at the edge of the circle. I will trust your word. I will tell you the direction. You trust my word. Then, if you win, you are free to go. The rules are simple, no punching, kicking, fishhooks, eye gouges, or groin strikes. We fight to the death."

"Counter, counter, counteroffer. We fight to the death or to unconsciousness. I will trust your word. You win, you take everything. But I still go free on my mission. Deal?"

"You trust that I won't kill you when you are unconscious?"

"I do," I said, thinking I really didn't have a choice if I was unconscious. But it did leave me a non-lethal out.

"Agreed," he rumbled.

I walked to the opposite end of the circle from him and removed all my weapons. Then I stripped down to just my Typhon Skin armor and necklace. "Acceptable?" I asked.

"Acceptable," he said, walking to a spot a little to the left of where walking straight would have led me, and ripped a small piece of bark from the tree. He placed it at a slight angle even more left. "There is your direction. Begin."

Okay, what is my edge? Let's see, he is bigger, taller, probably stronger, and obviously a superior wrestler since he was so anxious to have a wrestling match. Stamina? Maybe. This guy was impossibly large and no way he could go as long as I could. But if he was the wrestler that he appeared to be, he wouldn't tire quickly. Wrestlers and stamina are like dads and horrible puns, can't have one without the other. So, no real edge that I could see. I guess we'd have to do this the hard way.

We went back and forth for a minute or so trying various takedowns and holds. I surprised him with my strength, but he was faster than I thought possible, and stamina didn't seem to be an issue for him. Sure, he was tiring faster than I was, but he also wasn't still recovering from a plus-sized beating like the one I'd had yesterday. If this went on too long my speed advantage would be shot, and his strength advantage and superior wrestling were going to end this.

Superior wrestling. Yes! I could end this on my terms. It wasn't that wrestling had gotten all that much better since this guy's time, but the rules had changed. At least the rules as I was defining them. He was a classic Greco-Roman wrestler. I was going to introduce him to the Brazilian version. And no, I wasn't planning to shave him or anything gross like that.

The next time he shot in for a single leg I let him have it. When he came up for the pin, I wrapped my right leg around the back of his neck and pulled it down with my left leg. Then I pulled his head down in a classic BJJ choke that would be illegal in wrestling, but he'd never said, "No chokes."

I hoped that this would end things quickly as most people were lights out in a few seconds once the choke was applied. But I really underestimated his brute strength and the thickness of his neck. He managed to pick me up and body slam me back into the ground hard enough that I felt vertebrae crack. Somehow, I held on because if this didn't work, I was dead.

He managed to pick me up and slam me again but with much less force. Although that did not matter much because it was still an eight-foot drop. He couldn't lift me on the third try, and had started to sag, which was a good thing because I could no longer feel my legs. I had to reach up and pull my leg down with both hands to keep the choke going.

A few seconds later and I felt him lose consciousness. He didn't tap. I could respect that. If I held the hold a little while longer, he would be dead. I didn't, though. I rolled him to the side and thought about standing up.

Man oh man, I bet standing up would hurt. Fortunately, I couldn't, so I wouldn't have to know if it hurt as much as I feared. Instead, I did a few stretches to (hopefully) align my spine and allow the healing to start. I figured this was going to take even longer than the last fight. Seemed to be the story of my life. No wonder a wise man once said, "Nobody wins a fight."

After about five minutes, as I was just managing to roll unsteadily to my feet, he woke.

"I was out?" he grunted.

I nodded.

He smiled and it was a really nice smile.

I could like this guy if he wasn't so ancient. He looked to be at least thirty and I'm not into grandfathers.

"Well done, Miss Munchkin, well done. Only one other has ever bested me. Go in peace and good luck on your quest," he said, reaching behind a stump. I tensed but he only grabbed what appeared to be a small, silver coin and tossed it to me. I looked at it and it bore his likeness on one side, and two people beginning to wrestle on the other. "A parting gift for you . . . for the lesson."

He smiled again and I returned it and headed off in the direction he indicated earlier, thankful he was a man of his word. I barely had enough strength and control in my legs to manage to not stagger until I was out of eye and ear shot.

Then I slumped to the ground and massaged my legs until the needles in them faded to something a little more bearable. I also grabbed the last of my energy bars and ate them. If this trip went on much longer, I was going to be doing a lot of searching for protein, but I really needed the energy right now. My body was working so hard to repair the damage that I felt like I had a fever and my spine was almost on fire. I really, really needed to sit for an hour or so and just recover before I passed out entirely.

Instead of passing out, I decided to slog on and hope. *I heal really fast,* I told myself again. Even with that bold and daring pep-talk, slogging was a challenge. An hour or so later I was still feeling little random shocks in my legs, and occasionally stumbling as my spine attempted to heal.

I more or less kept staggering forward while hoping that I would be in at least acceptable shape before I got to town and hoping that getting there wouldn't take that long.

19
INTO THE CASTLE

So split the difference.

A couple hours later, sometime before sunset, I spotted a guard station a hundred yards to my left and a gateway entrance perhaps a quarter mile ahead. Now all I had to do was just sit and snack on nuts and berries that were also getting decidedly low and wait. And wait. And wait. And wait.

Okay, so it was probably only another hour or so but sitting there quietly feeling my spine knit together and my bruises fade was not very exciting. On the other hand, it was useful. A wise woman once told me that useful was usually enough.

Eventually a small caravan passed, and I slid in behind them and entered the castle grounds as if I was part of the group. I even followed them into town for a couple of blocks to get a feel for the town. It was not a happy place. While there was obviously more wealth and money here than in the smaller places I'd visited in this world, there was also more of a sense of unhappiness.

Buildings were anywhere from two to four-stories high and mostly made of stone. Windows appeared to be made of real glass. The people hurried about their business and barely spared a glance for anyone around them.

I know! The place reminded me of New York. At least the midtown part. You know, the part where everyone was scrambling for one more coin, one more score, one more . . . anything. They had no time to live because they were busy gaining things that were not really important. Daddy told me that was how he was before he met Mama.

Anyway, I eventually peeled off from the group at what was obviously an inn, which I cleverly deduced from the sign above the door that read INN.

The inside of the inn was small and packed tightly with eight tables, the ubiquitous fireplace with a small deer roasting in it, and a couple of stewpots simmering away. If I ever moved to this land, I was definitely going to start a stewpot franchise. It seemed every inn had more than one.

Anyway, I sat down on the far-right side of the room and took a load off my feet. I was the only one in there and it felt nice just to sit and relax. A few minutes later a serving girl came out of the back room. She looked just like the others, only better dressed. What do they do? Clone serving girls? She took my order of meat and cheese and fruit and wine—no way I was trusting the water in this city. She seemed surprised about the size of my order, enough to feed three grown men, but she quickly settled down when I paid in advance and tipped her well.

The food came out surprisingly quickly and was much blander than the meals I'd enjoyed in the smaller towns. Typical of big cities, very fast, very efficient, lower quality, and higher cost. I ate it all. There was no telling when I'd have chance to have another meal. Besides, I eat a lot. Get over it. Sorry, guys, but I can out eat you. Sorry girls, but I couldn't gain weight if I tried. The bulletproof metabolism of youth combined with super pills . . . or whatever, left me perpetually skinny. Okay, it probably was not the pills. I had experimented with not taking them since talking to the Seer and I hadn't noticed anything other than I get a LOT hungrier a lot faster.

After finishing my meal or three, I called the serving girl back. "You don't seem very busy," I said. "I am new in town and would like to pick your brain." She looked shocked and started to back away. "Wait!" I said. "That's just an expression where I come from. I am not going to touch your brain. I'd just like to know about the area." She still looked hesitant, so I took a silver coin out of my coin purse and placed it on the table across from me. Then I placed one next to it. As she walked toward me, I held up a gold one and placed it in front of me. "This one you get if I get the information I need, and I make sure no one knows who gave it to me."

She looked nervously around the empty room then scooped

up the silver coins. I stopped her. "Why don't you show me to a room? We can talk there, and no one will ever know we spoke." She still looked very hesitant, so I continued swiftly. "What I need won't get you in trouble, I promise, especially if you never talk to anyone about it. In fact," I said, tossing her the gold coin, "you stand to make quite of bit of money for a few moments of conversation about nothing."

I didn't really think all the cloak-and-dagger stuff was necessary, but she had the look of someone who had been waiting for this her whole life, and it really didn't affect me one way or the other.

She led me up to a private room in the back corner, closed the door, and looked at me with a sense of excitement. I looked around the room as if there could be spies listening in. Doubtful, since the only things in the room were a bed, wooden chair, nightstand, and small lamp, but the girl seemed to expect it.

"First, where can I find the Bull King?"

"Oh," she said, relieved and excited to have some information for me. "That one is easy. Walk down this street to the very end. You will find a large cave entrance. You really can't miss it. It has giant wood doors, and there is a sign above the doors that says 'Entrance.' There are always at least two guards in front to let people in. He is somewhere in the cave."

She leaned in and whispered conspiratorially, "It is said no one who has gone in has ever returned."

"Excellent," I replied. "Now tell me of the local gossip. Tell me everything." I leaned in and whispered, "I can't tell you why I want to know but I am certain you know enough about what is going on around here that I'll find my answers in our discussion." She gave me a knowing smile and proceeded to prattle on about things in which I had zero interest, but if anyone asked, she might not remember talking about the Bull King, or think it was that important.

Man, she talked a lot. It made me wonder if I talked that much. Probably not. Anyway, an hour later she ran out of steam and I gave her my thanks and got her promise not to tell anyone about our conversation. Then told her to listen to gossip in a week or two and she'd know everything. That seemed reasonable. Surely something would happen around town she could take credit for. I gave her the gold piece, bade her good night, wedged the chair against the door, and went to sleep for an hour. Again, I begrudged myself the rest, what with the potential I'd miss my deadline and all. I had no real idea if I'd already missed it. Dang you, Mobius! But I was going to try my best.

After a very restful, but all too short sleep, I woke, dressed, put my hair up in a fighting queue, rechecked and secured all my weapons and headed down for a quick meal. I know I said I didn't have to tie my hair up, but it does hurt if it gets pulled out and takes a little while to regrow. I hate looking like I have mange.

Anyway, a new serving girl brought me a large meal of leftover venison, egg, bacon, toast, jam, and juice. Then I had her bring me the same thing two more times. She was a little put off by the sheer amount but paying the bill and leaving a hefty tip seemed to put her back into a good humor. Seems like a large tip always has that effect. Who knew?

I made one stop on my way to the cave entrance. Starbucks, of course. I had a venti peppermint mocha since I was feeling festive. After all, with luck I would be going home tonight. Properly fortified and caffeinated, I finished my walk to the cave in over-sugared bliss.

The cave entrance was impressive: Two wooden doors, big enough to drive a wagon through, high enough that the wagons wouldn't have to be broken down, extremely thick, and shod with iron. There was a guard at either side of the gate. Each guard was dressed more ceremoniously than functionally in bright red tunics and blue trousers. Each carried a spear with a large blade affixed to its top, a sword sheathed on his left hip, and a dagger on his right. The blades were gem-encrusted and did not look used. Their boots were a blue that matched their shirts and looked uncomfortable to walk in, let alone fight.

Since there was no way to sneak past them and fighting should always be saved as a last option, especially when my legs were still twitching randomly, I decided to try the direct and friendly approach. I walked up to the guard on the left, stopped a few feet short so he would not feel threatened—and I was out of pike range—and spoke. "Um, hello?" Neither guard so much as glanced my way. "Good morning?" Nothing. "Looks like it's going to be a warm day? If you're happy and you know it stand there and do nothing?" Nothing.

I figured if they were not going to move, then there was nothing to stop me from entering so I walked toward the doors and pushed to open them. Nothing. I noticed a keyhole so that might be an issue. "Um, anyone have a key?" Nothing. "Hey, you idiots!" I screamed. "Open these doors so I can see the Bull King!"

One of them moved to the door, produced a key, and unlocked it. *I guess all I had to do was ask*, I thought, as the doors slid smoothly open.

I entered and the guards shut and locked the door behind me. There was no keyhole on this side so my only out now was through the other side. The room was fairly well lit even though there was no obvious light source, which was kind of cool. The room itself looked to be made of stacked stone and was maybe the size of a small bedroom. There was a person-sized door to the right and one to the left, and nothing else. I wondered for a second *Why have such large doors to the entrance only to have small doors immediately inside?* Then I wondered *Which door should I open?*

Suddenly, the ring I got from Ariadne burned sharply on the left side of my finger and I had my answer. *This is going to be easier than I thought,* I thought as I went and opened the door to the left. It was pitch black inside. No light from the room so much as entered through the doorway. Well, no problem there. *Modern technology trumps creepy old magic any day,* was my thought as I grabbed a flashlight from my go-bag. I turned it on with a smile. Then, of course, I immediately frowned as I noticed the light from the flashlight didn't penetrate the dark, either.

Crap. I guess sometimes magic wins. Just to be certain, and definitely not because I was playing with a cool trick while I should be charging forward, I shined the light back and forth a few more times. Yup, plenty of light in the room, no light at all going through the doorway. Looks like I'd be stumbling through the dark for a while.

Ten steps later my "for a while" almost ended as I took a step forward and started to fall into what was a pit of some kind. My falling foot came against the inside of the wall and I pushed forward as hard as I could, hoping to leap past the hole. I guess I partially succeeded, or I should probably say suck-ceeded, as my hands and my nose rammed into a wall about ten feet in the distance. There seemed to be just enough traction that I got barely enough grip with my feet to leap back and land on my back about a foot from where I'd fallen in the hole. I scrambled back another foot trying to ignore the wrenching in my back. It felt like I had re-cracked a disk or two in my spine. Oh, goody, just what I needed.

Well, no help for it. Hopefully, my back was just jammed or something and would heal before I found the Bull King. I hated the thought of going into the Final Battle at less than full strength.

Anyway, I walked back to the first room and opened the door across from it, ignored the burning of the ring, and entered. The hallway was well lit by apparently nothing again and I could see it ran at least a hundred yards straight before either ending, or coming to a T. It was too far down to the end to tell which one yet. I started down the hall and noted openings on either side as I made my way, looking for tracks, signs, or anything that would tell me which was the correct direction.

About halfway down, the ring started burning toward the left so I took that opening.

I was now in what looked like another mostly nondescript

hallway that ran in a roughly banana shape. Following it around brought me to a large, circular room. I'm guessing it was maybe twice the size of those UFC octagons you see on TV. That all would be harmless enough if it was not for the huge boar with oversized tusks standing in the middle of it, complete with a brass chest plate, shin guards, arm guards, and a leather skirt and boots. Oh, yeah, a spear in its right hand and a round, brass covered shield in its left.

20
HOP HEAVY

"Try to flee and I have no quarrel with cutting you down from behind."

Okay, a female monster, then.

"Well met, sister," I said as friendly(ly?) as I could. "I have no quarrel with you. Allow me to pass and we can part as friends. I can even tell the Bull King you fought valiantly."

She squealed with laughter. Get it? Squealed? Never mind.

"Even if I were to let you pass, you'd never find him. You couldn't have gone a worse direction or be more lost if you tried." She shook her head and grasped her spear more firmly. "No, little girl, I was promised ten deaths and I would be free. You don't look like much, but you will make seven." With that she lowered her spear and beckoned me forward.

Okay, how do you fight a hoplite? Or I guess a hop heavy, in this case. I shrugged out of my go-bag and drew two daggers. Let's see: She had the reach advantage, the strength advantage in all probability, and she was holding her spear and shield as if she was very comfortable with them. She admitted that she'd already killed six people, so she was a combat vet.

I had a positive attitude, legs that twitched randomly, and was already tired. Well, crap. Best case, this was going to suck. Seems like I'm saying that now almost as much as I say "anyway."

Anyway, I shifted one dagger down in my grip and charged in. As expected, she stabbed with the spear and I used my modified dagger shield to turn it aside, and as she was slightly off balance, I stabbed her spear arm.

Um, at least that was the plan. What really happened was I got a cut on my arm, managed to get inside her spear, and was slammed to the side hard enough by her shield to drive me into the far wall. Her shield was not just for defense, it was a pretty effective battering ram as well. I didn't even manage to nick her.

Time for a new plan.

Evidently, my new plan was to stay just ahead of her as she stabbed the spear at me repeatedly, keeping me at a distance. As plans go, it wasn't my best. I was managing little more than staying slightly ahead of her and picking up the occasional slice when she outguessed me. My armor stopped the majority of the cuts, but I was still getting the occasional one on my hands, face, and neck. So far, none of the cuts were in a place that would cause blood to run into my eyes, but it was close. I dipped, ducked, dashed, and dived. It was exhausting and I was starting to breathe hard after a couple of minutes. So was she, but it did not look as if she was tiring all that much faster than I was. I needed to end this quickly or she was eventually going to end it for me.

Desperation time. I threw my left-hand knife underhanded at her leg and, of course, it did nothing. That was not the point. Get it? Point? Geesh, why do I bother?

Anyway, what it did accomplish was getting her to lower her shield enough I could throw the knife in my right hand much more accurately at her throat. She managed to block that as well, but I was expecting worst-case at this point and had already leapt into her chest.

She dropped her spear and shield and closed both arms around me as I reached for the knives in my boots. I headbutted her and saw stars. I saw even more as she returned my headbutt with one of her own. By this point, I had a knife in each hand, and she had her arms around me, holding me tight. It was a race. Even though my hands were pinned I could stab her arms. Even though I was stabbing her arms she was squeezing tightly enough that I my already bruised back was failing rapidly. I was running out of breath, consciousness, and vertebrae to crack when I felt her grip loosen slightly.

I ducked my head so that when she went for another headbutt I got nothing more than a tusk slash that felt like it half scalped me. As I fell, I jammed both knives into her, one in each leg. She leaned slightly forward, and I managed to free one knife and force it through her throat. She collapsed on top of me and I was too far gone to do anything except lie on the ground with her weight pinning me down. I passed out and hoped she bled out before getting enough strength back to kill me.

Evidently, she did, bleed out, that is. I was covered in pig blood and had a large hop heavy draped over me when I awoke an indeterminate time later. It took all my available energy to roll her off me and I sat up slowly, then made my way shakily to my feet.

Let's see, back feeling like it was recrushed, check, scalp hanging partially off, check, entire body bruised and battered, check, knee dislocated—how did that happen? Check. Okay. I put my scalp and knee back into place and stretched my back as best I could. I assumed the fresh pain and needles in my legs were a good thing, because I couldn't do anything about it so it might as well be good. Then I went to my go-bag to devour the rest of my food. It was not going to be enough to heal me when I was this far gone, and I was going to be starving in an hour or so, but I needed those calories now. I scoured the room but found nothing other than a wine skin filled with sour water which I drank dry. What did she eat?

Anyway, I took her spear more to use as a walking stick than anything else because my legs were shaking again. Then I examined the two doors in the room. The ring was burning to the left, so I opened that one and was immediately hit with a spring-loaded club that knocked me back across the room and broke a bunch of my ribs. Well, maybe a couple were just cracked so I had that going for me. While I sat there putting ribs back in place it finally occurred to me. The ring was telling me where the danger was. Idiot!

I staggered back to my feet and went to the door on the right. It opened and there were two options. The ring burned on the right and I went left. Then it burned left, and I went right. Rinse and repeat.

21
THE BULL KING

Less than an hour later, I entered a large throne room with (obviously) a large throne. Sitting on it was an even larger bull. And I know that is a lot of larges, but the room was huge, maybe the size of a basketball court, and the throne looked like Shaquille O'Neil would get lost in it.

And the bull? Well, he was not really a bull, but a giant of a man with a bull head. I estimated he was close to nine feet tall, with well over eight hundred pounds of solid muscle. He was wearing leather armor from neck to waist, a short loin cloth, leather boots, and nothing else.

He stared at me for a moment with a puzzled and slightly amused look before speaking. "Well met, little warrior. No one has been to see me in years. I was seriously beginning to doubt you would make it here, either." He looked around with a wry smile, which is just odd on a bull face. "Of course, I am a bit hard to find. But you'd think my friends would find a way. But enough of my musings. How may I be of assistance to you?"

I needed at least a day to fully heal, and judging by the ridiculously long and heavy one-handed, well-worn sword leaning against the throne, that might not matter. This dude was a serious warrior. Well, I needed a day, so taking a few moments to converse could only help.

"I have come seeking a boon, Noble King."

He stared at me. "Yes?"

I smiled with glee. "Oh, thank you! That will make everything so much easier," I said, knowing it would annoy him, but I couldn't help myself.

Oddly enough, he did not seem all that annoyed. He laughed a loud and joyous laugh before responding, "I meant 'yes,' as in continue, little warrior."

"Oh, I see," I said, feigning understanding. "Well, you see, *giant warrior*," I said, trying to enforce the irony on the words "giant warrior." I was getting tired of the "little." I mean, sure, I was, and maybe he meant it as a compliment, but still. "It seems every seven years you kidnap, eat, and return the bones of children from my world. I have come to ask you to stop."

"I see," he said and then shook his head. "Unfortunately, I cannot stop. I am cursed. I can no more stop taking your children than I can stop breathing."

"Your words sadden me. If you can no more stop killing children than stop breathing, it appears I am going to have to help you stop breathing," I concluded, while readying the spear to throw. I figured I might as well get some use from it.

He stopped me with a wave of his hand. "A moment, little warrior. You seem like a good person and I would hate to kill you."

"Nope. No way," I responded vehemently. "I am not ripping off the *Princess Bride* here."

He laughed heartily again. "A true film buff, I see. I am surprised that one as young as you has seen it. But that was not my point. My point is you cannot kill me. Part of my curse is I cannot die. I cannot die, and I must kill."

"No offense, Your Majesty, I know your kind is known for honesty, but I cannot simply take your word for it. I did not come this far only to say, 'Oh well,' and walk away."

"I see your point, little warrior—"

"Munchkin. Call me Munchkin."

He nodded. "You may call me Minos. Well, then, Munchkin, we seem to have come to an impasse. However," he said, looking me over from head to toe, "I seem to have you at a major disadvantage. You are barely upright, and your legs are shaking. I do not believe you are afraid, so I am going to guess you injured your spine rather badly. Merely getting to my chambers has nearly killed you. I would give you time to rest and heal, but it honestly appears you are months away from full strength . . . if you ever get back to it. I have no doubt you are a mighty warrior, little one, but you are asking for a fight you cannot win."

I couldn't argue with his logic so I cleverly said, "Well, I cannot argue with your logic, Minos, but I do not have months to heal. Unless of course you can stop abducting and eating children until I do heal. Maybe at least give me an extension? Say, one month?"

"Sadly, I cannot," he said, and actually did seem sad. "What do you suggest as an alternative, Munchkin? Even if you kill me, which I think you would find impossible even at full strength, I really do not wish to die. And even if I wished to die, my curse will not allow it."

"I see," I said, seeing, "and is there a way for you to die?"

"There is."

"And will you tell me this way?"

"I would normally say 'no', but you interest me, Miss Munchkin. Or is it just Munchkin?" I nodded. "Very well, Munchkin, there is a way to kill me. I cannot be truly harmed

216

by normal weapons, or even most magical ones. It would take something very special to end my curse."

"I see," I said, seeing again, "and will you tell me what weapons will harm you?"

"I said you interest me, not that I am suicidal. Even though I have doubts about your ability fully healed and with the right weapon to kill me, I see no benefit to me in taking that kind of chance."

"I see," I said, getting tired of saying that. "So, it looks as if I am going to have to try to kill you with just what I have on me. I can only hope your information is incorrect. Weapons have come a long way, you know. Allow me to reach into my bag and I will demonstrate."

"Oh, please, by all means," he said with a huge smile on his stupid bull face.

Well, hopefully, I was about to shut him up permanently. I reached into my bag for my bow and a couple of hunting arrows.

He stood up and laughed at me and I put an arrow into his armor exactly where his heart should be. As the forced rocked him back slightly I put another arrow through the same hole. He dropped to his knees, hung his head and looked down and my heart nearly burst with unanticipated joy.

Then he reached for the shafts with both hands and snapped

them off close to his armor. He stood up, leaned forward slightly, sucked in his chest and shook a little, and as the bent and spent arrow points fell out under his armor he smiled, and said, "Ow."

Double crap. I was in some serious trouble. Seems like that ought to be my motto. He reached to his right and drew his giant freaking sword from its sheath and began to walk toward me. "Prove yourself worthy, Munchkin. Prove yourself and you will be rewarded in this life or the next."

I picked up the spear and charged, really hoping my reward would be in this life. And . . . success! He was surprisingly slow! *Ha!* I thought as I easily dodged his thrust and rammed the spear that I had braced into my shoulder into his leg with everything I had.

Unfortunately, my happiness was short-lived as this did not go well. The spear stopped suddenly at his leg and the shaft broke, not only dislocating my shoulder, but also ramming a broken piece of wood in my cheek. The pain was excruciating, nearly more so than the backhand he hit me with that slammed me to the ground and quite possible broke my neck. He might be slow, but he was definitely strong.

"Yield," he said and placed the point of his sword to my throat. "Yield and I will show you mercy."

My response was to bat the sword away with my good hand

and roll to my feet. Since this required rolling across my broken shoulder I saw stars, but at least my legs seemed to be mostly working, so half full. Or maybe only a quarter full. There were anywhere from two to three of him in front of me now, so it appeared I had a concussion—again. Without thinking, I jumped back out of his range.

Thank all that is holy he was slow, so the sweep of his sword missed my neck by inches. I backed up quickly and took a breath. He did not even bother to pursue me, so I took a second to check my cheek, which was really hurting. There was a piece of wood through it, scratching my gums. It didn't look like pulling it out was an option, so I pulled it the rest of the way through. Gross, and ouch!

He had politely waited the entire time. When I looked at him again there was mostly just one of him and it was motioning me forward.

"Whenever you are ready, Munchkin," he said politely. "I am in no hurry to kill you."

Time for a new strategy.

I walked over to the spear and snapped off the head. Then I broke it in two and had a half stick in each hand. I dodged and weaved, using my far superior speed and technique until he made a clumsy thrust and gave him my best Mike Trout into his right leg and spun away. He was limping as he came after me. I maneuvered around him and after his next clumsy thrust, I hit him in the side of the knee again. He fell to one knee and I hit him in the head with everything I had. He dropped onto his back and my club snapped in two. It was now worthless for anything but stabbing so I stabbed him in the leg. Nothing. No penetration, it just stopped like I'd tried to stab a wall. All it did was give him enough time to slam a fist into my sternum. Even from his back it was hard enough to nearly crack my sternum and fling me back onto my butt which hurt . . . a lot.

I got slowly to my feet and he lumbered to his and began stalking me again. He was limping hard and favoring his leg so I figured I had a good chance to end this if I could find a way to actually penetrate his skin. Maybe through the eye hole? Those are rarely armored. His lids looked like they were just skin, not dragon scales or anything.

Plan made, I continually circled toward his good leg until he over committed with his big old sword and spun to slam the inside of his bad leg again. As he staggered back, I kicked solidly between his legs which darn near broke my shin but did leave him on his knees with his hands held low protecting what most boys will protect at all costs. I took a quick step forward and drove my stick straight into his right eye to end this once and for all.

Except it did not penetrate. It rocked his head back and I did it again. And again. Nothing. I was getting tired here. It's not like he had the skill to hurt me so long as I was careful, but I had no idea how to permanently take him down; and I was getting tired, and my body was filled with a gazillion bruises. I lunged again because I had no better idea and the stick broke. So, I jammed the broken stick into his eye. His only response was to slug me in the chest again. He had more leverage so this time I flew back a few feet farther before landing on my bruised tailbone.

As I scrambled to my feet, he lumbered to his and held out his hand, palm facing me. "A moment please, I need to catch my breath."

I had nothing to lose as I needed a minute or so as well, so I nodded and took a step back. I drew two of my daggers and waited. I had little hope of them accomplishing anything, but something was usually better than nothing.

He looked at me and laughed. After a few moments of solid chuckling he spoke. "Oh, you are worthy, Munchkin. You are worthy. It seems we have reached an impasse, though. You are clearly the superior warrior, but you cannot truly harm me. I have been unable to penetrate your defenses enough to seriously hurt you. I propose a succession of hostilities long enough to discuss a bargain."

I had nothing to lose, so I simply said, "Agreed. You don't

mind if I ready another arrow or two while we talk, do you?"

He shrugged. "If it makes you feel better, please do. Those arrows really cannot hurt me."

Man, his confidence was unnerving. I grabbed my bow and a couple more arrows just in case we couldn't reach an agreement, and he was wrong about being pretty much impossible to kill. While I was grabbing them, he limped back to his throne, using his sword as a cane, and sat down with the sword across his knees. I noticed his sword left little puncture marks in the stone. Good thing I hadn't let him hit me with it.

Well, back to the matter at hand. Armed and as dangerous as I felt I could be, I walked to about ten feet from the throne and waited.

"Sit, please, Munchkin. I promise that no matter the result of our conversation, hostilities will not resume until you are ready."

"No, thank you," I said. "I prefer to stand." Actually, I was tired enough that I debated my ability to get back to my feet if I sat on the floor. I was really not in good shape. Sure, things were knitting back together, but not at my usual breakneck (pun intended) speed. I was not going to heal enough to finish this. And my body was beginning to burn muscle in an attempt to heal me which would certainly start cramps soon. And then, sadly for me, I would die.

"Well, Munchkin," he said, rubbing his sore leg, "you certainly made it more interesting than anyone has made it in as long as I can remember." He paused. "So, I offer you this bargain. We quit trying to kill each other now, and I tell you how you might actually hurt me."

I frowned. "And what is in it for you? You do seem to have the advantage now. Why give me a chance to heal and come back with a weapon that would allow me to actually kill you?"

He nodded. "A perfectly good question and well asked. Though there are undoubtedly more, I only know of two weapons in this land that can hurt me. There is the sword Beowulf used to kill Grendel, but its owner is a fighter from legend. While perhaps you can best him, that is a very chancy thing. Besides, I will not give you his location."

"And the other?" I asked.

"Occam's razor. It is said it can cut through to the heart of any matter, or being," he said with a wry smile.

"And why tell me this?" I asked.

"It is simple, Munchkin," he replied, "I have nothing to lose by giving you this information. To get this razor you will have to retrieve it from one of the greatest sorceresses in all the lands. One, I doubt that you can retrieve it from her. So, you will be dead and there will be no more battles between us. Two, if you do retrieve the razor, it will most certainly be that you retrieved it by killing her. If you kill her it might release me from my curse, which will mean there will be no reason for animosity between us, unless I decide to start a non-cursed killing spree, that is."

Since I could not win at this time, I had nothing to lose. "Where do I find this sorceress?"

He frowned. "I honestly do not know. She was missing for some years, but word is she recently returned somewhere in a distant land. I know no more." He smiled. "Do we have a deal?"

"Um, sure," I said, relieved because I was going to be dead if we fought again today. "One condition. You kill no more children until I retrieve the razor. Then we can talk again about our arrangement."

"Agreed," he said. "But, unfortunately, I can only give you two weeks."

Let's see, two weeks to travel through an unknown world, toward an unknown location, and kill an unstoppable opponent. Well, I'd done two and a half of the three already. "You have a deal."

TO BE CONTINUED